THE CRYSTAL'S CURSE

Also by Jane Alden

Jobyna's Blue

Across A Crowded Room

THE CRYSTAL'S CURSE

Jane Alden

Desert Palm Press

The Crystal's Curse

By Jane Alden

©2020 Jane Alden

ISBN (book): 9781948327947
ISBN (epub): 9781948327954
ISBN (pdf): 9781948327961

Desert Palm Press
1961 Main Street, Suite 220
Watsonville, California 95076
www.desertpalmpress.com

Editor: Heather Flournoy
Cover Design: TreeHouse Studio

Printed in the United States of America
First Edition December 2020

Acknowledgements

Many thanks to editor Heather Flournoy. She held the author's hand from beta reading through final editing. She is thorough, affirming, objective, and knows when to stand her ground. The Crystal's Curse is far, far better because of her help.

Ann McMan's cover elevates the story behind it. She captured the haunting eternal presence of Hatshepsut, one of history's strongest and most successful leaders. Thanks, Ann.

PROLOGUE

THEBES, EGYPT 1458 BCE

THE FILIGREED BRONZE LAMP sputtered, and Senenmut picked it up and shook it. Plenty of oil. He pinched the wick, and the glow brightened a little and steadied. He blew out a breath in frustration. He had just fired the royal palace's Chief Supply Officer for diluting the lamp oil supply, selling the excess on the black market, and pocketing the money. Could the new man be doing the same? Of course, the problem might be that Senenmut's eyes were getting old.

He stretched and yawned. He could not sleep, so he decided he might as well get some work done. He moved the light closer to the papyrus picturing decorations for the walls and ceiling of his tomb. He gave one more thought to the oil. He must remember to do a surprise inspection of the supply in the morning.

Raucous laughter from the banquet hall echoed down the corridor. He recognized the voice of Thutmose, the twenty-one-year-old stepson of the King. He and his generals would revel all night.

From sunrise this morning, the kingdom had celebrated Thutmose's triumph over the Hittites with a military parade through the royal city and a feast. At dawn, a thousand of the bravest warriors, three hundred horse-drawn chariots, and five hundred horn players and drummers marched between Karnak Temple and Luxor Temple. The procession stretched the mile and a half down the Avenue of Sphinxes to file past King Hatshepsut, seated on her golden throne in front of the Temple of Luxor, between two obelisks bearing her name and the story of her anointment by Amen-Re as ruler of the two kingdoms.

Senenmut had viewed the spectacle from a place of honor, seated on King Hatshepsut's right hand. He was her architect, confidante, and her most trusted advisor, closer to her than anyone—even Useramen, the vizier.

At the very end of the procession, Thutmose's gold chariot stopped in front of the Pharaoh. Her young nephew appeared resplendent in a pharaoh's battle helmet of lapis and gold. He was bare to the waist of his short linen kilt. A wide gold collar called attention to his well-muscled bare chest. He drove his own chariot, though he never would have done so during battle. No doubt he wanted to show off his skills as a horseman. The crowd of a hundred thousand Thebans responded with a sustained roar that sounded like thunder.

1

Senenmut had ignored the show, which he found garish and tasteless, and focused his attention on his beloved King. She sat perfectly still and straight, her face showing no emotion, but Senenmut could read her thoughts. She wondered if she'd made a mistake appointing her stepson commander of the Egyptian army. Senenmut knew she had her reasons, and the arrangement benefited the kingdom. Thutmose was more successful than any warrior pharaoh before. In only five years, he conquered the hated enemies to the north.

Hatshepsut's trouble with Thutmose began twenty years before. Thutmose II, Hatshepsut's husband and brother, died with only two heirs. Hatshepsut was of royal blood, but a woman. His son was only half royal and only one year old. She became regent for the boy. Then came the blessed day everything changed. The Gods anointed Hatshepsut Pharaoh and lord of the two kingdoms.

At first, the boy's advisors were the lone voices questioning the validity of a female King. As Thutmose matured and gathered supporters, he raised his own questions. To keep him occupied, Hatshepsut sent him north to fight the Hittites. Now he had returned, a full-grown man and a hero, beloved by the crowd.

Another shout from the rowdy crowd in the banquet hall echoed down the corridor, calling Senenmut away from his musings. He opened his door and peered to the left toward the door of the King's quarters at the end of the hallway. Something was off. There was no sentry on guard. Could the fool have abandoned his post to drink with the revelers?

Senenmut hurried down the corridor toward the King's apartment as quickly as he could, cursing the pain in his arthritic knees. The door flew open and a white-faced chambermaid stood in the archway, her mouth frozen in a silent scream. He knocked her aside and rushed through the bedchamber to the bath.

Hatshepsut floated naked in her tub, face up, below the surface. Fragrant steam rose lazily from the water. Senenmut knelt beside her, ignoring the pain in his knees and the water covering the stone floor. He lifted the Pharaoh's head gently to the surface. Her dark eyes were wide open, the pupils fixed. At the base of her neck, two angry purple bruises marred her coffee-colored skin. Her expression was serene and regal. She saw Death coming and decided to submit gracefully. Her left arm lay across her bare breasts, bent at the elbow in the traditional pose of a royal mummy. Positioning the King thus was either the murderer's gesture of respect or a cynical joke.

The chambermaid had followed him into the bath, and she found her voice and began screaming. He rose, grabbed her shoulders, and shook her hard. "Where were her attendants?"

"She sent them away, except for me. I was preparing the fire in the brazier for the night, in the bedchamber with my back to the door. I didn't see anything. I swear." She slumped to the floor. "I'm dead, too."

***

The clay lamp sputtered. Senenmut remembered the same sound on the awful night three months ago when Hatshepsut died. On that night, the lamp was ornately carved bronze, and the lamplight shed shadows over gilded furniture of exotic woods and intricate wall paintings in his rooms in the royal palace. Very different from this cellar where he was hiding, under an abandoned mud brick hut.

A sound, a slight rustling outside in the street, caught Senenmut's attention. He blew out the lamp flame and leaned his ear against a crack between the bricks. He held his breath, listening for the rattle of weapons and whispered commands. The royal guard would come for him soon. Secrets didn't last long in the workers' village where he had taken cover, near the tombs and temples of the Valley of the Kings.

No more sounds. His hand shook as he re-lit the lamp. The light was a risk, but he must finish his mission before the new pharaoh's henchmen came for him. He went to the corner of the room, removed a loose brick, and pulled out a large, oblong crystal. He returned with the crystal to a rough-hewn wooden table on which rested a papyrus, pen, and ink. He was writing Hatshepsut's *Book of the Dead*. The document provided magic spells to hide her from hostile forces and help her through the underworld and into the afterlife.

He held the crystal up to the lamp and beams of light spangled the dirt floor and mud brick walls. The *Book* also gave detailed directions for using the light from the crystal to find Hatshepsut's new resting place. The god Wepawet would need to know so he could guide her soul on the journey through the underworld.

He took up his pen and waited for his hand to steady before signing, *By the hand of Senenmut, noble, beloved of his lord, in life under the Mistress of the Two Lands, King of Upper and Lower Egypt, Hatshepsut, who liveth forever.*

He started to carefully roll the papyrus, then stopped and took up the pen again. *To him who disturbs this crystal with evil in his heart, death shall come on swift wings.*

Satisfied, he placed the papyrus and the crystal into a small rosewood chest, closed the lid, and sealed it with Hatshepsut's royal cartouche. Now for his last act of devotion, he must hide the chest near Hatshepsut in her new secret resting place.

Senenmut blew out the lamp and slipped out the door and across the main street. A full moon hung in the night sky over the workers' houses. He crouched as close to the ground as his old knees would allow and scuttled to the shelter of the shadow cast by the wall surrounding the village. He ran south along the wall to the point where it made a turn east toward the banks of the Nile. He stopped to check for movement on the road. All was quiet, and he headed toward the white colonnaded terraces of Hatshepsut's funerary temple, perched halfway up the hill and shining in the moonlight.

To the right of the temple, on top of a steep embankment, a pile of sand and rocks marked the entrance to his unfinished tomb. He paused for a moment, reliving the best day of his life when Hatshepsut honored him by designating his tomb site near her temple. He carefully picked his way up the steep embankment, along the path workmen took to carve his final resting place from the living rock of the brown mountain. Twice, he almost slipped in the loose sand and rocks. By the time he reached the entrance to the tomb he was out of breath, and he stopped to rest a moment.

Since he knew every inch of the construction, he didn't risk lighting a lamp. He felt his way along the wall of the narrow corridor that led down through the vaulted anteroom and into the unfinished burial chamber where he placed the rosewood chest in a niche. He stopped in the anteroom, knelt, and whispered a last goodbye to his beloved King. He felt his way up the entrance corridor, guided by the moonlight shining in the entrance.

He walked back to the village and down the middle of the main road toward his cellar. No need to hide now; his duty had been done. A figure stepped from the shadows. His spotless white ankle-length linen skirt glowed in the moonlight, and his shaved head was bare of the customary black wig. He carried a staff topped with a gold cobra head, the official symbol of the King's vizier. "Greetings, Senenmut." He looked up at the moon. "A nice night for a stroll."

"Have you come alone for me, Useramen? I expected you'd bring men with weapons."

"The royal guard will come tomorrow." The vizier looked up and down the deserted street. "Will you invite me in, or must we talk in the street?"

Senenmut led Useramen down the steps and inside. He lit the oil lamp again and offered the vizier his only chair, seating himself cross-legged on the dirt floor. "If the royal guard comes tomorrow, why are you here tonight?"

"I've come with a gift." The vizier took a small blue glass vial from the waistband of his skirt, placed it on the edge of the table, and slid it toward Senenmut.

"Why are you offering me this gift?"

The vizier laid his staff of office carefully on the table in front of him. "Let's talk frankly, my old friend. You have committed treason against the Gods and King Thutmose III. You have stolen Hatshepsut from her consecrated resting place and hidden her. The punishment for your crime is death. You've heard the same stories I have about Thutmose's treatment of the vanquished Hittite chiefs. I suspect he intends your death to be both public and painful." He stroked the golden head of his staff. "She was my King, too, and I know you served her well. Thutmose finds me useful now, but who can say for how long? When it's my time, perhaps someone will show me mercy."

Senenmut picked up the vial and turned it in his hands. "Will I be buried in my tomb?"

"It's not my decision, of course. If you tell Thutmose where she is, confess your treason publicly, and disclose who conspired with you, perhaps. If not, they will seal your tomb forever, unfinished and empty."

Senenmut nodded and smiled. Hatshepsut would be hidden and safe forever. He pulled the stopper from the vial and drank the poison down to the last drop.

Chapter One

NEW YORK CITY 1972

I GUESS YOU COULD say that my story begins the day I first heard the name Cassandra Stillwell. I'm Ari Morgan, by the way, twenty-three years old from Beaufort, North Carolina. Just so you know, it's pronounced Bow-fert, not Byew-fert like the town with the same name in South Carolina. This is a sore point for North Carolinians, so consider yourself warned. Or, at least informed.

Some people would call my upbringing "redneck." I would say "sheltered." That changed with my acceptance to Barnard after high school. Barnard's location, in the middle of New York City right across the street from Columbia, attracted me to apply there in the first place. We didn't have to spend our time on campus isolated in a boring small town. The city supplied part of our education. The Upper West Side of Manhattan was our version of a college town. If you were looking for a place with a ra-ra spirit, it wasn't for you. Barnard was for anyone who wanted independence, which described me to a T. Also, we got discounted or free tickets to movies, plays, and museums. Call me cheap.

That morning, I crossed the grassy area in front of Milbank Hall, stepping through an obstacle course of sunbathers, trying to avoid casting my shadow on anyone. The key in the palm of my balled-up fist felt slippery. I had been unconsciously gripping it like a totem, as if I hung on tightly enough, things would change.

Across Broadway from Barnard College, a clock tower on the Columbia campus began chiming eleven o'clock. I opened the heavy double doors of Milbank Hall and took the stairs two at a time to Dr. Eleanor Frame's second-floor classroom. I watched through the glass as she paced confidently in front of the blackboard then turned to emphasize some point she was making with a bold, slashing chalk line underneath the phrase "Symbolism in Mrs. Dalloway."

Eleanor had earned her reputation as an expert on Virginia Woolf, and she was proud of her accomplishments in the academic world. Her classes were always full. Today, twenty or so students—all women except one guy sitting in the back row—hung on her every word. I recognized the looks on their faces–slightly parted lips, small smile, glazed eyes. Adoration of Dr. Frame. The same expression I wore just a year before.

What could possibly motivate the lone guy to take "Modernist Women Authors in the Early Twentieth Century"? One of the great things about Barnard was you could be attending a small women's college while still having access to Columbia across the street. The students at Columbia had the same opportunity to take Barnard classes, but the men hardly ever did, and this guy didn't look like a Virginia Woolf fan.

The end-of-class buzzer broke the spell, and people began gathering their books and leaving. I stood outside as the guy stopped to flirt with Eleanor. That explained what he was doing in the class. He was barking up the wrong tree was what he was doing. I actually felt sorry for him. Just for a moment.

Eleanor turned and began erasing the blackboard, talking to him over her shoulder, a dismissive signal he finally picked up on, to my relief. He nodded to me on his way out, and I stepped around him and inside the door. "Hello, Eleanor."

She stopped erasing the board in mid-swipe. "Ari."

"I brought your key." I slapped it down on the desk, harder than I intended, making a comically loud pop that caused us both to jump. "Sorry." I lined the key up squarely alongside her briefcase. "I got all my things out, so..."

She looked around the empty classroom before reacting. "Oh, babe. You could have left the key in the apartment."

"I guess. Didn't think of that."

She checked her watch. "It's a little early, but do you want some lunch, or maybe some coffee?"

I didn't, but I did.

"Are you done with finals?"

I nodded.

"Let's get some coffee."

Outside on the grass, a sunbather sat up, leaning on an elbow and shielding her eyes with one hand. Alison. One of my roommates. "Hi, Ari. Hi, Dr. Frame. Ari, will you be around tonight? We're toasting the Class of Seventy-two." She pretended to hide her mouth from Eleanor. "With champagne."

I nodded. "I'll be there."

Eleanor steered us toward the campus gate off Broadway. "Let's go across the street to Columbia. More privacy." She glanced at me while we waited for a break in the traffic. "Does she know about us?"

"Not from me, she doesn't. She's not stupid, though. She may have noticed I don't spend many nights in the dorm."

"I thought she gave me a knowing look."

I'd miss a lot about my six-month affair with Eleanor. I started making a list in my head. Number One: She was hot as hell. Underneath the silk blouse and A-line skirt, tastefully accessorized with a set of perfectly matched pearls, she had the body of Wonder Woman. We passed a plate glass window, and our reflections followed us down the sidewalk. The couple in the window brought up Number Two on my list. Even though Eleanor looked ultra-graceful and feminine, and my oxford cloth shirt and penny loafers would be most generously described as "tailored," she was in charge. She was the top in bed. She decided what we did and when we did it. I loved that paradox.

And the all-important Number Three. Everybody wanted her and, for a while anyway, I had her. Call me shallow.

But I could also make another list of what I wouldn't miss. Number One: She was paranoid that people like my roommate Alison would find out about us, even though it was common knowledge that every semester she took on an acolyte to worship at the altar of her wonderfulness. It was practically an item in the freshman orientation handbook. The fact I got picked, during my senior year, gave me some standing among the lesbians on campus. Again, call me shallow.

We never went anywhere together in public. We spent all our time in her apartment, a really swanky one on the Upper East Side on 96th, overlooking the park. She acquired the place in a divorce settlement. We stayed in bed or read aloud to each other or worked out in a room furnished as a fully equipped gym. After a semester of our affair, I was a lot more sexually sophisticated, I was beginning to understand Gertrude Stein, and I was in the best shape of my life.

Against my will, my mind skipped back to the list of things I'd miss. Number Four: She was really smart, and also really funny. When I told her I was starting to get Gertrude Stein's prose, she said, "Alice B. Toklas wrote in her journal, 'This has been a most wonderful evening. Gertrude has said things tonight it will take her ten years to understand.'" Eleanor may be the only person in the world who knows that quote and finds exactly the right time to toss it into a casual conversation.

Listing the good and bad wasn't a good way to make me feel better about the breakup. I tried to create Numbers Two and Three, et cetera, of things I wouldn't miss, but came up empty. She was pretty great, and she never misled me. She was clear from the beginning about what our relationship meant to her. It had a shelf life of a few months.

Some metal café tables with spindly legged chairs, mostly unoccupied, sat across from the coffee cart. We took our coffee to one of the tables. She leaned toward me with her forearms braced on the tipsy table. I recognized the crease between her brows signaling her tension. "Babe, are you all right?"

Number Two on the dislikes list: "babe." I hated her calling me that. I moved the table a little, trying to find a steadier spot for it. "No, but I will be."

She searched my face, then blew out a breath and took a sip of her coffee.

I decided to let her off the hook. "I'm starting the creative writing program in September at Columbia, thanks to your helping me get the tuition grant."

"That was easy. You're a wonderful writer."

"Thanks. I'll get a summer job, probably in the library again."

She opened her briefcase and took out a piece of cream-colored note paper, folded in half. She tapped the paper against her thumbnail. I could see the wheels turning in her head. She was weighing whether to show it to me or not. "I may have an idea for your summer." She made up her mind and handed it to me.

It was heavy paper, the kind you'd find in a little shop on Madison Avenue where you wander in some Saturday afternoon, look around, and ask yourself, "Who in hell would pay this kind of money for paper?" I unfolded it. On it was written in a bold hand, *Cassandra Stillwell* and a phone number.

I tossed the paper back on the table between our coffee cups. "Who's she?"

"She's an acquaintance of mine. A visiting professor at Columbia. She's looking for an assistant for the summer, and she asked me if I knew anyone. I told her I might."

"What kind of an assistant?"

"She's an archaeologist, quite a well-known one. She's going to Egypt in a few days and she wants a helper to go with her."

"Why would you think of me? I don't know anything about archaeology or Egypt."

"You're a wonderful writer and detail oriented, and your main job would be keeping a careful record of her work, sort of a scribe. Also, you'd be a good temperamental match for her. You're levelheaded, and Cass is unconventional and...intense."

"Intense how?"

"She's quite brilliant, I think, but she has some unusual theories about research in archaeology. She challenges some commonly held ideas about the subject, but don't ask me any details. I'm out of my depth. I met her socially. I get the impression she doesn't mind upsetting the grey-haired white guys in her discipline."

So far, Eleanor was listing reasons Cassandra Stillwell should pick me to go with her to Egypt. Why did she think working for this archaeologist would be a good idea for me? From Eleanor's point of view, my being in the middle of the Sahara Desert halfway around the world would serve one purpose for sure—this job would get me out of town and off her conscience. Out of sight and out of mind.

"Why should I consider it?" I took some sadistic pleasure making her sweat a little.

She picked up the phone number and absent-mindedly unfolded and refolded it. "It's entirely up to you, of course. A summer in Egypt would offer great material for your writing. It would be an interesting experience and useful on your resume. You don't want to go home to North Carolina for three months, do you? And you hated working in the library last summer. Putting myself in your shoes, if I were your age and graduating with three months looming before me, I'd at least meet her."

I took the paper out of her hand. Whatever Eleanor's motive, the job might be something to consider. Could be a win-win for both of us.

"Maybe I'll call her."

"Good." She leaned back in her chair and sipped her coffee. The pearls settled into the crevice between her perfect breasts. She followed my gaze to her chest. "Would you like to come to the apartment for some dinner tonight? Or are you committed to champagne with your roommates?" A confident smile played around her mouth.

I wanted to and I didn't want to. I put off a decision. "Can I call you later? If I'm going to contact Cassandra Stillwell, I should do it now, before she finds somebody else."

"Of course." She was surprised I hadn't jumped at the chance to be with her. Her shrug had a studied nonchalance to it. Good enough.

I left Eleanor to finish her coffee. I walked back across Broadway and found a quiet bench to sit on and analyze the pros and cons of possibly spending the next three months in Egypt with a woman Eleanor called intense. I could go home for the summer with my mother and grandmother in North Carolina. They'd love having me there, and Beaufort might not be so bad. I could get some kind of job. Summers in high school I used to dress up like a pirate and conduct the Pirates and Ghosts tours for all the tourists. Beaufort was Blackbeard territory.

I got a picture of Egypt's pyramids and sphinxes. Much more exotic and alluring. And Eleanor knew what she was talking about. Going to Egypt with a well-known professor at Columbia would look great on my resume. If Cassandra Stillwell wanted a detailed-oriented assistant, that was me. Also, I was intrigued by Eleanor's description of her as unconventional and intense.

The pros won. I found a pay phone and dialed Cassandra Stillwell's number from the fancy paper. I felt disappointed when her answering machine picked up. Once I decided to try for the job, my competitive soul kicked in. I'd be her best choice for an assistant, and she needed to know that fact before she made some other decision.

"Cassandra Stillwell here. If you require a ring back, please leave your number." Her low-pitched voice with a posh-sounding British accent left the impression she was indifferent whether you left a call-back number or not.

I recorded a message, mentioning Eleanor's name and leaving the number of the switchboard at our dorm. By the time I got back across the Quad to Hewitt Hall, a pink message slip stuck out of my mailbox. "Miss Morgan, meet me in Room 115 at the Met Museum at 11:00 tomorrow morning. Cass Stillwell."

***

Identical lighted reading lamps on double ranks of study kiosks created unbroken lines stretching to infinity in the main reading room of Butler Library. There were two people in the cavernous space, me and the library assistant dozing with his chin propped on his hand at the reference desk behind me. A week ago, the last study time before finals at Columbia, every chair would have been occupied. Butler was affectionately known as The Butt, which is the part of your anatomy that got numb from sitting too long in the hard-wooden chairs. The Butt was the only library on the Columbia/Barnard campuses that stayed open all night the last weeks of the term.

Cassandra Stillwell's phone message sent me to the library for an all-nighter, boning up on ancient Egypt. There would be no intimate farewell dinner with Eleanor. Probably for the best.

The tiny desk in front of me was covered with back copies of archaeological journals and oversized hardcover books. After I got a sort of general knowledge from the books, I started looking up articles authored by Cassandra Stillwell. She sprang on the academic scene ten years before as a second and third author in the British journal of the Royal Archaeological Institute.

Over the next five years, she wrote a steady stream of research articles, one every two or three months, becoming more focused on pharaohs of the New Kingdom. She moved up to first author, and her articles found their way across the pond to the *American Journal of Archaeology*. Then a funny thing happened. Two years ago, she wrote an article entitled, "Murder in the Valley of the Kings." She had published nothing after that.

The article was about what Stillwell described as the mysterious death, 3500 years ago, of a female pharaoh I'd never heard of: Hatshepsut. I wasn't sure how to pronounce her name. Aside from the infamous Cleopatra, I never even knew there were female pharaohs. I scanned the introduction. Stillwell laid out a case that Hatshepsut didn't die from natural causes, but that she was murdered. The summary didn't finger any particular suspect but asserted further research could identify the killer.

There were photographs at the end of the article showing hieroglyphics. I couldn't read them, of course. In one of the photos, Stillwell held up a stone fragment for the camera and pointed to a figure, probably Hatshepsut. Stillwell didn't look like I'd expected. I thought she'd be something like Deborah Kerr in the old movie *King Solomon's Mine*, in a pith helmet with a long gauzy scarf dangling down her back. She was darker, more youthful looking, and thinner, with long black hair tied in a ponytail at the nape of her neck. The rolled-up sleeves of her khaki shirt showed sinewy muscles in her forearms. From all the digging, I figured.

The next mentions of Stillwell in the index of periodical literature were in editorial comments by outraged archaeologists critical of her research methods and conclusions. They asserted Hatshepsut was not pharaoh at all, but only regent for her young stepson, Thutmose III. Therefore, they reasoned, he had no motive for a murder.

You could practically hear the sputtering indignation as they pointed out the mummy of Hatshepsut had never been found. All the critics were male except one: Dr. Helena Bendix, Associate Professor of Egyptology at Oxford. She accused Cassandra Stillwell of writing a pulp fiction novel, not a well-researched scholarly work.

"Hey."

I jumped a mile, spun around in my chair, and came face-to-face with the library assistant. His royal blue cotton vest with the Columbia logo sagged on his sloped shoulders. It could have used a turn through the washer. His hair was on the greasy side and hung in his eyes. "Are you done with some of these?" He gestured toward the piles of books and magazines. "I get off in half an hour, and if you decide to walk out with all these scattered around, I can't leave until everything's put away."

"Oh, sure." I started stacking the books and magazines. "I need to copy this article." I held up the journal with the Hatshepsut piece.

He glanced over his shoulder at the clock hanging above the reference desk. "You could steal it."

"What?"

"Kidding. Do me a favor and wait till the next guy comes on. The copier has to warm up and everything."

This bozo reminded me why I didn't want to spend the summer working in a campus library with the likes of him. I needed to get an assistant job with Cassandra Stillwell.

Chapter Two

THE GREAT ENTRANCE HALL of the Metropolitan Museum of Art echoed with noise from a large crowd of tourists, art students, and New Yorkers, shuffling docilely past two guards checking admission tickets. I had visited the Met many times. Free admission, remember? But I hadn't paid much attention to their Egyptian collection.

One of the guards eyed my student ID, handed me a map of the exhibits, and waved me through. Room 115 was directly to the right. I was half an hour early on purpose. I wanted to look over the Hatshepsut exhibit and read through my resume one more time to check for typos. I also wanted to observe Cassandra Stillwell when she arrived, before she saw me.

She was there already, alone in the cavernous exhibit hall. At least I was pretty sure this woman was Stillwell from the photograph at the end of her journal article. In place of the khaki shirt, she wore a white silk blouse over a straight black skirt, which would have been ordinary looking except for the slit up the side to just above her knee showing off her killer figure. She wore her dark hair in a bun, unlike the more casual hairdo in the photo at the end of the journal article.

Cassandra stood in front of a massive granite statue of Hatshepsut in the formal seated pose of a pharaoh. She was dressed as a male in a kilt, naked to the waist without breasts and with a fake beard. I had seen photos of this particular statue. Someone in ancient times took a chisel to the figure, chipping off the cobra and vulture from her crown and the royal crook and flail she once held in her lap.

Stillwell's head was bowed, her eyes were closed, and she silently moved her lips. I got the very creepy feeling she was carrying on a conversation with the statue. She began quietly humming some melody I couldn't quite make out. I tiptoed to my right, to a marble bench against the opposite wall, and waited. After a couple of minutes, a ray of sunlight broke between the clouds and beamed through the skylight, illuminating the stone face of the pharaoh. Again, creepy.

Stillwell raised her head and took a few steps backward, away from the pharaoh. "Are you Ari?"

I jumped up. "I am. Sorry, I didn't want to interrupt your..." Conversation? Prayer? Song?

Thankfully, she turned toward me and offered her hand before I had to find the right word. "Cassandra Stillwell. Call me Cass. I wasn't sure it was you. I expected a Middle Eastern person from your name, Ari."

I stepped forward to shake hands a little too fast and a little too close and almost bumped knees with her. "Ari is short for Ariadne."

She cocked her head and looked me over. "Oh, so you're Greek?"

"No, Irish. My mother was reading a book on Greek mythology the day I was born."

"Well, Ariadne, meet Hatshepsut." She made a sweeping gesture that took in all the statues and artifacts in the gallery. "At least some of the earthly representations of her. I've always found it ironic that her exhibit is in an art museum. Hatshepsut didn't consider these statues art. She had a very practical purpose for them. Public relations. They were the TV commercials of their day."

An image jumped into my head of a TV ad showing a helicopter shot of a crowd of people on a hilltop singing about wanting to buy the world a Coke. Will that commercial wind up in the Metropolitan Museum of Art some day?

"Hatshepsut wanted to keep her pharaonic image in front of people, to keep reminding them she was divinely anointed by the god Amun as ruler of the two kingdoms."

"She's dressed as a man. Was she trying to pass?"

Cass laughed. "No, but her gender was secondary to her role as ruler. There were simply no words or images in ancient Egypt to depict a female pharaoh, so she adopted the male ones."

"Just a minute." I dug in my bookbag for a pen and tablet and began to take notes. I could tell Cass was used to giving lectures about the female pharaoh.

"She ruled during the Eighteenth Dynasty of Egypt."

Cass pronounced the word *dinn-asty*.

"She sat on the throne for twenty-two years, carried out the most ambitious building program the world had ever seen, reestablished trade routes dormant for hundreds of years, and opened up the flow of gold from the Southern Kingdom. Then she was murdered because she was a woman."

"Wow!"

"Right. But we have to prove it, and to prove it, she says we have to find her."

I looked up from my notes. *She says we have to find her.* I didn't know which part to be more surprised about—that Hatshepsut spoke to her or that she said "we" had to find her. Did she mean me?

"So, you're saying this is an expedition to Egypt to solve a thirty-five-hundred-year-old murder?"

Cass stepped closer to the statue, and her finger traced the outline of the chipped-off royal flail.

I swallowed a gasp, expecting some museum attendant in a black uniform to materialize and throw us out for touching the exhibit.

"Are you a rule follower, Ariadne?"

She must have heard my gasp. I felt my face go hot. And I wished to hell I hadn't offered up my full first name if she was going to insist on calling me Ariadne.

She waited for an answer. I had to tell the truth. Might as well. I wouldn't want to get the job under false pretenses. Guess my compulsion for the truth would confirm me as a rule follower. This was the weirdest job interview I had ever done, which is saying a lot. I once tried out for a trick waterskiing team in Florida. Part of the job application was climbing up on the shoulders of nine people to the top of a skiing human pyramid.

Before I could admit to being a rule follower, she went on. "Eleanor implied as much. She also said you're levelheaded. I could use someone levelheaded. She may have told you I'm a little unconventional."

"She also called you intense."

"Oh, she did, did she?" Cass' husky laugh came from her diaphragm. Very sexy. She didn't mind Eleanor's characterizing her as intense. She took it as a compliment. "Well, that's true. You might as well know all my warts. I believe archaeology is mostly intuitive, more an art than a science. I spend a lot of time listening to voices inside my own head. I'm told I can come across as moody and glum."

"We all get moods."

"For days at a time."

"Oh."

Outside the exhibit hall, indistinct murmuring and shuffling grew louder. A crowd of Japanese tourists ambled in, headed by a female guide walking backward and holding up a furled umbrella. She led the group to a statue against the back wall of the room. It was a representation of a kneeling man holding a plaque covered with hieroglyphics. The guide gathered in the stragglers, and once they were all clustered around, she began a lecture in Japanese. She must have been quite the standup comedy talent, because the crowd interrupted her talk often with uproarious laughter.

Cass groaned and sighed heavily.

"Who is that statue? What's so funny?"

"It's Senenmut, Hatshepsut's chief architect and strongest supporter. I don't speak Japanese, but judging from the group's reaction, she's repeating a salacious and completely false story about his being Hatshepsut's lover and the father of her only daughter."

Cass motioned toward the door. "Let's get out of here." We went through the Grand Entrance Hall and out the museum's front doors. Scattered couples and individuals reclined on the steps listening to a flute player and violist performing for spare change. We found a quiet corner.

"Now, where were we? Oh, yes, we need to find Hatshepsut. Are you familiar with hieroglyphics? No matter if not. You can copy them competently with a little practice. Drawing them isn't the hard part. It's interpreting them, and that's my job. You'll learn a lot about their meaning, too, in the process. You will keep a minute-by-minute journal of our dig. This kind of consistent attention to detail is not my strong suit. When time comes to prove our case about Hatshepsut's murder, there must be no room for questioning the methods and results."

I guess I had a deer-in-the-headlights look, because she stopped. "Have I overwhelmed you?"

"No, no. But maybe you'd like to know more about me? I have a resume here explaining my education and experience as they might relate to success factors—"

She held up her hand. "I know all I need to know about you."

"Well, I know you've heard about me from Eleanor. She knows me pretty well." You might say really well, I thought to myself. "But she and I didn't exactly spend a lot of time talking about—"

She shook her head. "My assessment doesn't come from Eleanor." She gazed at the double line of yellow taxis moving sluggishly down Fifth Avenue. "You're from North Carolina, probably the coastal area. Your father died young, I suspect in the Korean War, before you could have known him, yet you feel close to his memory. You are attending Barnard on a scholarship, and you feel responsible for taking advantage of your fine education to better your mother's life."

Surprising tears sprang up behind my eyes. Cass took my hands in hers. Her touch felt strong, like her forearms looked in the photo in the journal article.

"How do you know all this?"

"I told you about my intuition. I also pay attention to clues. People in the coastal area of North Carolina have a distinctive accent, a holdover from British settlers. The way you pronounce vowels is different, and you drop the 'r' after vowels."

"I've worked on changing my accent."

"Don't. Be proud of your heritage." Cass turned my hand over. "The ring you're wearing is the most important clue. The tan line shows you wear it all the time. The band says, 'Beaufort High School.' A small town in North Carolina, right?"

She pronounced it right. I nodded.

"About your father, you wear the ring on the middle finger of your right hand. Since you're right-handed, it's your largest finger. The ring must have originally been sized for a man. The date on the ring is 1947, about twenty years before you would have graduated. I also see the outline of a set of dog tags under your sweater. Were they his?"

I nodded again. I tried blinking back the tears, but I was losing the battle. Cass took a tissue from her pocket and handed it to me.

"Do you want me to go on?"

I didn't know if I did or not. Cass' examination made me feel like I was standing in a police lineup in my underwear. At the same time, there was something liberating about the feeling that she really got me and was still willing to consider me as her assistant. "How do you know I'm on a scholarship?" Even my roommates didn't know that.

"Barnard is expensive, and you are very careful with your spending. When you wore out the soles of your shoes, walking instead of paying for cabs or even the subway, you had them re-soled. I imagine your father's early death has something to do with your parsimony." She shrugged. "Two plus two."

I wrote in my notebook *Parsimony? A nicer way to say cheap?*

Cass stood and drew me up with her. "Decision time. We have only a few days to get ready. I know you possess the 'success factors,' as you call them." She ticked them off on her fingers. "You're careful. You arrived early to prepare for our meeting. You've been taking notes the whole time. We've established you're a rule follower. All these things I am not. So, Ariadne, will you come with me and help me find Hatshepsut?"

To buy a little time, I put my notebook and my carefully crafted resume back in my bookbag. No opportunity to do a proper pros and cons list. I had to make a decision on the spot whether to follow this unusual woman into the unknown. I held my nose and jumped in. "Yes."

"Brilliant!" She drew me back down to sit on the steps. "Now, we need to get busy. I want to be in Luxor no later than two weeks from today. You'll need a passport. Unless you have a passport. Do you? And you'll need a visa. We'll go straightaway to the Egyptian embassy."

"Wait." I held up my hand to stop the barrage of words and took out my notebook to start a list.

"A list. Good." She looked down at my loafers. "Do you have boots? You're going to need some good boots. And a hat. We'll go to Lord & Taylor. They have a whole department." She already knew I couldn't afford to even walk in the door of Lord & Taylor, so she was going to buy me a wardrobe? She stood up, brushed her skirt, and headed toward the curb to hail a cab. "Let's go, Ariadne."

I ran to keep up with her, juggling my bag. "Cass, can I ask one thing?"

"What?"

"Could you call me Ari?"

Chapter Three

"MOM."

"ARI. I'M SO glad you called. Your grandmother has been worrying me to death to call you. I just never know when it is a good time."

I felt a little stab of guilt. I had been putting off calling my mother to tell her I'd be going to Egypt with Cass for the summer, trying to think of how to drop this bomb without worrying her. "How is Gran?"

"Just a minute, honey." I could hear the crackle and static of the phone as my mother struggled to stretch the cord from where it hung on the wall in the kitchen to a quieter place on the back porch. "Sorry, honey. She's got 'The Price is Right' cranked up so high I can't hear myself think. Why do you suppose Bob Barker insists on holding that skinny little microphone when nobody else on TV does anymore?"

"I don't know. Security blanket, maybe."

"Well, you didn't call me to talk about Bob Barker. How are you, dear? Are you and your friends all excited about graduation exercises? I wish your gran and I could come, but we just went through another bout with her sugar diabetes flaring up, and I don't think we can even consider a trip right now."

"It's okay, Mom." I took a deep breath and decided I'd have to come out with it. "In fact, as it turns out I won't be here for the ceremony. I'm leaving in four days for Egypt."

"Egypt?"

"Yes, I have a summer job in Luxor, Egypt."

"Isn't there a war going on in Egypt?"

"That was five years ago, Mom, and the fighting only lasted for six days."

"But there's always a war going on somewhere over there, or one about to start. Aren't the Russians in Egypt?" The pitch of my mother's voice rose higher with each question.

"Yes, but the president just signed a peace treaty with the Russians."

"I know, but all the same..."

I pictured her on the back porch of our little white wood-siding house, across the street from the United Methodist Church and the Old Burying Ground. She would be nervously fingering the hem of her apron as she tried to figure out how to deal with all this disturbing information and not seem like an over-controlling mother. I heard the scrape of a wooden chair being dragged across the floor. "Are you all right?"

"I'm just sitting down. What in the world kind of a job do you have in Egypt?"

"I'm going to work with a famous archaeologist, a woman. Dr. Cassandra Stillwell."

"You're going to be digging in the desert?"

"Well, I don't think I'll actually be physically digging. I'm going to be a sort of assistant and record keeper. We'll be searching for a lost female pharaoh, Hatshepsut."

"Hatshepsut." She slowly repeated the unfamiliar syllables. "Wait a minute. Let me get a pencil and write this down. Hold on."

I heard the rattle of spare batteries, mismatched keys, loose change, and paper clips when she pulled out the "holds everything" drawer in the kitchen. "Hat-shep-sut and Dr. Cassandra Stillwell." She was quiet again, absorbing everything. "How will I keep track of you while you're all the way over there? I don't expect you can call us. Too expensive, not to mention the differences in time zones. Your gran will be worried."

"I've thought of that. I'll write to you every night. Once the pipeline gets full, you'll hear from me daily, and I can call you every other week or so."

She tried to make her voice cheery. "It sounds interesting and...different."

"I didn't have time to tell you I was interviewing for the job. The whole thing just happened, and I had to decide right away."

"This Professor Stillwell. Would I be able to look her up at the library? Gran is going to quiz me on every detail, and I want to be able to answer her questions." She hesitated. "I'm curious, too."

"I have an article Dr. Stillwell wrote about Hatshepsut. It's got her biography at the end. I'll send it to you today, and Mom, can I ship a box of stuff home for the summer? I'll give some of it away, or toss it, but most of my clothes won't be of much use in Egypt in July and August."

"Of course you can. You'll be able to come home and get them, before you start Columbia in the fall, right?"

"Definitely." I slid down the wall to sit cross-legged on the linoleum floor of the cramped, stuffy little cubbyhole that served as a phone booth on the fourth floor of my dorm. Someone was always stealing the stool.

"I'm going to send you a twenty-dollar bill in the mail."

"Don't do that, Mama. It won't get here before I leave."

"But you'll need things. You'll need a hat. I've seen pictures in the *National Geographic.* It's very sunny in Egypt. Do you have a hat?" That made me smile. Both my mother and Cass were worried about the welfare of my Irish skin. Cass and I spent two hours the week before in Lord & Taylor, and I walked out with bagsful of boots, scarves, khaki pants and shirts, and a cool sunhat. "Yep. All set."

"Oh...well...do you want to speak to Gran?"

"Don't interrupt her show. I'll write her a letter as soon as we get there. We fly to Cairo on Thursday, then on to Luxor."

"I suppose your Professor Stillwell knows what she's doing."

"Yes, Mama, she does."

"And I won't tell you to be careful, because I know you will."

"I love you, Mom."

"We love you. We're so proud of you. Don't forget us."

"I won't. I'll see you in a few weeks."

Chapter Four

CASS PICKED SEATS FOR us in front of the huge plate glass windows at the Gate 36 waiting area. We watched jumbo jets, one after another, back away from gates along the concourse and taxi toward the outbound runways. I chewed a hangnail and tried concentrating on the book I'd brought, *Egyptian Grammar: Introduction to the Study of Hieroglyphics*. I figured by the time we got to Luxor twenty hours after takeoff from JFK, I could have memorized a good chunk of the 800 ancient Egyptian alphabet characters. I fully expected nerves and excitement would keep me awake the whole way.

I didn't tell Cass this would be my first plane ride. No need for her to know exactly how big a hayseed I really was. My longest trips before were the Greyhound bus rides between North Carolina and the Port Authority Bus Terminal in New York City. I stole a sideways glance at Cass.

She held a briefcase in her lap. It was made of soft brown leather, closed with a strap and a gold buckle with a lock. It looked very expensive. She had propped an archaeological journal against the case and was sedately flipping through the pages. "Is this your first plane trip?"

Damn! How did she do that? "Yes, it is."

"Quite auspicious for your first one. Are you nervous?"

I squirmed in the hard-plastic seat. They certainly didn't go to any trouble to make passengers comfortable, and maybe less nervous. "Yes, I guess I am a little."

She nodded and closed the magazine. "Don't worry. We'll be there before you know it." She surprised me by reaching over and embracing me. I felt a tingle in the pit of my stomach. She was a really good hugger. You know how when some people hug you it feels awkward and uncomfortable, and with some people it feels like a perfect fit? She felt like a perfect fit. I wouldn't have guessed it. "I know. Let's make a list to calm you down."

"Great." I dug my notebook out of my bookbag, opened it to the first blank page, and put the date at the top. I waited for her to pull a calendar or her own notes from the briefcase, but she left it closed and locked on her lap and stared out the window.

"Number One: Meet Alfi outside customs in Luxor."

"Who's Alfie?"

Cass looked at my notes. "Not Alfie. A-L-F-I. Mohammed El Alfi. He's my first lieutenant for the dig. He recruits the workers, designs and builds the support structures, supervises the day-to-day work, translates for me, and keeps me from making terrible cultural gaffes."

"He's your Senenmut, like Hatshepsut's most loyal follower."

Cass didn't respond. She passed her hand over the briefcase in her lap, stared out the window, and hummed under her breath the tune I'd heard in the museum. Was she communicating with King Hatshepsut at that moment? I hoped my offhand remark hadn't put her in one of those moods she mentioned. What should I do? When in doubt, go back to the list. "Number One: Meet Alfi. Number Two: Check in to the hotel?"

"Yes. We'll have time to freshen up a bit before meeting the Ministry of Antiquities representative. She's coming to Luxor from Cairo. Dr. Hala Tarek."

How would I ever remember these names? They didn't exactly roll off my North Carolina tongue.

"She's responsible for issuing dig permits. Our search for Hatshepsut will have some controversy attached to it, so it's important we get her support for our project."

"What kind of controversy?"

"In general, the Egyptians are sick and tired of the stuffed-shirt academic British and the rich and acquisitive Americans going to Egypt, tomb robbing, and taking ancient treasures out of their country. They rightfully want to keep their history in Egypt for their own people, but the Egyptian Museum in Cairo has always been pitifully substandard."

"Why?"

"A story as old as the treasures themselves: gold and greed. In the past, the Ministry of Antiquities had problems with bribes and favoritism at the highest levels. The government is trying to eliminate the corruption."

"How will you convince Dr. Tarek we're different from the other Americans and British?"

"My purpose is not to steal Hatshepsut away. We're not financed by Americans or anyone else, and I've given up striving for academic recognition. I want to restore the truth of Hatshepsut's reign as the greatest ruler of the two kingdoms, male or female, and solve her murder. Her stepson tried to take her true accomplishments away from her after her death. Some people want to deny her murder and the campaign against her memory."

I remembered the snide comment from Dr. Helena Bendix about the pulp fiction novel.

"That skepticism makes searching for Hatshepsut especially controversial."

The PA speaker, located directly over our heads, popped and boomed out, making us both jump. "Ladies and gentlemen waiting at Gate Thirty-six for Lufthansa Flight Four-six-seven to Cairo with a stopover in Frankfurt. We'll start boarding in just a few minutes. Please have your boarding passes available, and please stay seated until your section is called."

Cass gathered her things. "So, Number Three on our list: Charm Dr. Tarek and get our dig permit. A good agenda for our first day. Are you still nervous?"

I wasn't. Cass was right; making lists calmed me down. I scrambled to start a new one before stowing my notebook. I wasn't sure yet what to call the new list, maybe Possible Problems. The first entry was *Dr. Hala Tarek.*

Chapter Five

WE RAN THROUGH THE maze of the Frankfurt airport to make our connection. Thankfully, passport check was carefully organized with designated lines, everyone quietly waiting their turns with their passports open to the correct page and with the right answers ready. Cass took the lead, and since she knew what she was doing, we found our new gate with plenty of time.

After the wide-awake eight-hour flight to Frankfurt, I was finally able to sleep through the four hours to Cairo. The bump and skid of landing gear on the runway shook me awake, and I wiped my mouth in case I had drooled the whole way.

"Did you have a good sleep?" Cass leaned over and pulled the brown leather briefcase from underneath the seat in front of her into her lap. "We have one more leg to Luxor. Just an hour."

Cairo airport was totally different from Frankfurt. It was chaos. Passport check was more like a mob than the orderly lanes in the German port. Cass took my hand and pressed forward. I kept saying, "Excuse me, excuse me," as we pushed past women dressed all in black with their heads and faces covered and men in ankle-length cotton robes. Apologies didn't seem to matter to anyone, one way or another.

The flight to Luxor was like old home week for the men passengers. They stood in the aisle the whole time, ignoring the seat belt announcement, yelling at each other in Arabic, and hugging each other. American and Europeans' reverence for rules like standing in lines and buckling your seat belts didn't mean much to Egyptians.

The flight south from Cairo to Luxor followed the Nile. I was sitting in the window seat, and Cass leaned across me to point out landmarks below. The two top buttons of her soft silk blouse were undone. She was wearing a necklace, some kind of a gold charm hanging from an impossibly thin gold chain. I tried not to leer. Okay, maybe I have a bit of a breast obsession.

I scooted a little toward the window and focused on the river. From this height, it was a ribbon of blue with green strips on both sides bordered by the yellow sands of the Sahara as far as the eye could see. The colors were so stark and primary that it could have been a page out of a comic book.

Cass put her hand on my back. "Beautiful, isn't it?"

I stole another peek at her cleavage. "Yeah."

The pilot made an announcement in Arabic and turned on the seat belt sign, which didn't mean a thing to all the men standing in the aisle. They kept up their gesturing and yelling at each other right through landing.

Mohammed El Alfi met us at the gate. His smile when he saw Cass was radiant. "Dr. Stillwell." He pumped her hand in both of his. He was short for a man, not any taller than Cass, and dressed in a dark suit and tie.

Alfi appeared to know all the baggage people as intimately as brothers. More yelling in Arabic and hugging. Our bags magically came out first, and he piled them in the back of a small white van parked at the curb. Cass took the shotgun seat, and I crawled into the back.

The road into Luxor was two lanes laid out as straight as a string. On either side, only yellow Sahara sand with no vegetation at all. The outline of Luxor shimmered like a mirage in the distance. The inbound lane was crowded with motor scooters, tiny three-wheeled cars, and donkey carts piled high with sugar cane. Alfi steered our van into the empty outbound lane and floor-boarded it.

Once in a while a vehicle appeared on the horizon coming toward us in our lane, and Alfi scooted the van over to the middle so the truck or whatever had just enough room to whiz by. I squeezed my eyes shut and prayed. Cass showed no concern. She rolled her window down and let the hot air blow her hair.

We got into town at rush hour. Anyway, I supposed it was rush hour. Maybe the roads were always this crowded. Alfi honked and steered the van around four tourists in a horse-drawn carriage. I gripped the edge of my seat as three full-grown men sharing one motor scooter darted around us and weaved away through traffic. I rolled my window down, and the sounds and smells of Luxor's streets assaulted my senses. Dozens of car and scooter horns echoed off the buildings lining the narrow street. The horns didn't sound like American horns. They sounded more like ambulances, and I kept looking behind us, hoping we could stay out of the way.

Alfi's thick curly hair blocked my view to the front. Out the side windows, I could see we were coming into a street market. The air wafting into my face smelled of a complex mix of unfamiliar spices, fish, and raw chickens displayed on outdoor tables lining both sides of the road. The food smells, mixed with the odor of horse poop and dust and combined with the heat, were making me a little sick.

Traffic slowed to a crawl. It seemed all half million Luxor citizens—were they called Luxorites or Luxorians?—were out shopping for the evening meal, middle-aged men in ankle-length white cotton dresses, teenagers in jeans and T-shirts with the names of sports teams or American rock and roll groups, and women, covered in black from head to toe. How did they avoid heatstroke?

Cass checked her watch. She had rolled the sleeves of her silk blouse up to the elbows, baring her forearms. It reminded me of her hot picture at the end of the Hatshepsut journal article.

"Will this traffic let up soon, Alfi? We meet Dr. Tarek in an hour."

"Oh, yes, Dr. Stillwell." He turned his head to answer her question, and I had an anxious moment, wishing he'd keep his eyes on the road.

"We'll be through the market in another block or so and into Temple Plaza. Wider streets and people in more of a rush."

Cass looked at her watch again. "What do you know about Dr. Tarek?"

"She is very important, the number two person in the Ministry. I've heard she is young and ambitious..." Alfi glanced at Cass again. "And a zealot about protecting Egyptian cultural heritage."

"Good. She and I should get along just fine. I'm a zealot, too."

The narrow road opened onto a paved traffic roundabout with three lanes circling a stone obelisk. Alfi was right about people being more in a rush; cars and motor scooters appeared to take the lane markers as mere suggestions rather than rules. It made no sense to me, but Alfi was unfazed and steered our little van directly into the melee without even considering yielding to oncoming traffic. I closed my eyes and gripped the seat again. I opened one eye to peek around Alfi's head as the traffic circle spun us out an exit headed toward the Nile River. Across the river, the west bank, lined with green, shimmered in the distance. Behind the line of trees rose the ochre-colored arid hills of the Valley of the Kings, sacred burial place of the pharaohs. That's where Cass said we'd find Hatshepsut.

Chapter Six

THE LOBBY OF THE Winter Palace Hotel was blessedly cool after the sweltering, bustling streets outside. The marble mosaic floors and soaring three-story atrium over the elegant reception hall were impressive, but I felt a little disappointed. The lobby looked like pictures I'd seen of fancy hotels in Europe or even New York. I'd expected something more exotic and foreign, more sphinxes and pharaoh statues.

A young man in a cutaway coat and striped cravat came to attention and bowed deeply as we approached the enormous, elaborately carved reception desk. His name tag read "Evening Manager Samut Paneb."

"Dr. Stillwell, we are delighted to have you again. Your customary accommodations are ready for you."

"Hello, Sam. Meet my assistant, Ari Morgan." She gestured toward his name tag. "Evening Manager. You've gotten a nice promotion."

He colored under his dark skin. "I have, and much of the credit is due to your kind words about me to the owners during your last stay. My family and I are forever grateful."

"Well deserved."

While Cass checked us in, I wandered across the lobby, scanning the people lounging in overstuffed leather chairs, reading newspapers or simply waiting. I used the time to practice noticing details about people like Cass did. By the end of the summer I might be able to learn how she could read people so well.

The room was about three-quarters full. Men in light-colored linen suits with stiff collars and ties smoked and read newspapers. Some were accompanied by women in gauzy summer frocks. Most appeared to be Americans or Europeans. A couple caught my attention. He was middle aged with salt-and-pepper hair and a neatly trimmed mustache. He wore the same light-colored suit. Nothing unusual.

The woman was a different matter. The most striking thing about her, what caught my attention in the first place, was her astonishing hair, rising in a feathery cloud above the top edge of the newspaper she held in front of her face. When I was seven, my grandmother bought me a wonderful Christmas present—a box of a hundred crayons, all different colors, many I had never even imagined before. My favorite was burnt umber, sort of a dark orange. I became obsessed with that crayon. For weeks, I colored burnt umber trees, burnt umber houses, and burnt umber dogs. Behind her newspaper, this woman's hair was a startling shade of burnt umber.

The newspaper was the *London Times. English speaking, and probably British not American.* I doubted many Americans read any papers other than US ones. A large, black, furled umbrella leaned against the arm of her chair. There wasn't a cloud in the late-June sky, so I figured the umbrella was for shelter from the ferocious sun. *She spends significant time outside and she has sensitive skin.*

I edged a little closer to the couple. Then I felt someone watching me from across the room. You know how sometimes you can feel someone staring at you? It was a man, studying me as closely as I was studying burnt umber lady. He wore a dark suit and tie and looked Middle Eastern. When our eyes met, he didn't glance away but casually took a puff off his cigarette. Creepy.

"Ari." Cass' voice echoed across the lobby. She held up her passport and beckoned me over to the reception desk. She needed my identification for registration.

I gave the burnt umber lady a last glance. She had lowered her newspaper and was squinting toward the sound of Cass' voice. *Nearsighted, but too vain to wear glasses.*

She jumped up, knocking over her umbrella, and shouted, "Cassandra Stillwell? Is that you, Cassandra?"

Still holding the newspaper, she rushed across the lobby to Cass. "I thought I recognized your voice." She wagged her finger in front of Cass' nose. "So, you've decided to come out of hiding finally. We haven't seen you in ages. What brings you to Luxor this summer?" She asked the question with a pert smile, but it came out sounding confrontational and intrusive. "Still Hatshepsut, I suppose?"

The two women stared at each other silently for an awkward moment. Cass put her arm around my waist and drew me to her side. "Dr. Helena Bendix, Ariadne Morgan, my assistant."

Helena Bendix! She was the woman who wrote the negative critique of Cass' Hatshepsut research.

"Ariadne, is it?"

"Ari."

"You must meet my assistant, Arthur Timms. I'd say you and Arthur have a lot in common, but unless you like to avoid work at any cost, you probably won't. He's around here somewhere. He wanders off and heaven knows where he goes." She leaned in. "I suspect he cruises the market." She said all this without even looking at me. Her attention was glued to Cass.

Bendix gestured toward her companion across the room. "We've just arrived ourselves, Lord Dysart and me. You must let me introduce you." She leaned closer to Cass and whispered, "I'm sure you know of him. The largest private collection of New Kingdom antiquities in England, maybe in the world."

She continued in a low voice. "Lord Dysart's an amateur, of course, but very earnest. And very generous." She touched a dark green glass scarab necklace at her throat. The sacred beetle was encased in gold and suspended from a gold chain. "Come and meet him." She pulled Cass across the lobby, and Cass pulled me along with her.

"Lord Dysart, this is Dr. Cassandra Stillwell."

He closed the magazine he was reading, an archaeological journal, and rose to take Cass' hand. "Dr. Stillwell. Call me Peter, please. Of course, I know your work. Hatshepsut, right?"

"Yes. This is my assistant, Ariadne Morgan."

Lord Dysart nodded at me and turned back to Cass. "I've read your research with great interest." He shook his head and chuckled. "'The Woman Who Would Be King.' Our collection at Hammond House focuses on the New Kingdom as well. I'm quite proud of having managed to amass antiquities representing the entire period from 1550 to 1070 BC." He looked around the lobby and leaned in conspiratorially. "Things have been especially challenging during this latest round of the Antiquities Ministry's increased regulations against serious private collectors like myself." He sighed. "Oh, well. We must persevere. Did Helena tell you what we're onto in the Valley of the Queens? She thinks we might come across Nefertiti."

Helena fidgeted with her necklace again. "You mustn't give away all our secrets, Peter, especially since I suspect Cassandra wouldn't give up any of hers in exchange."

Lord Dysart touched Helena's arm. The gesture seemed a little too intimate and familiar. I glanced at Cass to see if she'd noticed. Of course, she had.

"Nonsense, my dear. We're all colleagues here, right, Dr. Stillwell? We're making progress on securing our dig permit from the Ministry. So far, the Minister of Antiquities appears a very accommodating chap, but Helena is concerned his Number Two may be a different matter."

Helena nodded. "I have to meet the dragon tomorrow afternoon. Dr. Hala Tarek. Do you know her?"

"We haven't met." Cass was being very careful about giving the two of them any details.

Lord Dysart beamed at Cass. "And what about you? What will you be working on this summer, Dr. Stillwell? No doubt more about Hatshepsut?"

Cass backed away toward the reception desk. "Helena's right. We must keep our secrets. Well, we'll finish checking in. Good luck to you both."

I glanced toward where the man in the dark suit had been sitting. He was gone.

Cass completed registration, and we gathered our smaller bags and headed for the elevator. Cass checked her watch. "Bloody hell. Now we're really rushed. We meet Dr. Tarek in half an hour."

"Dr. Bendix called her the dragon. What did she mean?"

"I'm not sure yet."

The elevator operator held the door. He was dressed in a red jacket with gold braids all over the front and a turban. Finally, something in the Winter Palace Hotel fitting my picture of Egyptian exotic. As we were about to step into the elevator, Helena rushed up. "Cassandra, I hope you didn't take my little comments in the *American Journal* personally. I may have overstated a bit, but you know you must catch the editors' attention to get in print."

"Actually, Helena, your comments were among the more benign. I'm still getting outraged letters from our male colleagues. You would think Hatshepsut had personally impugned their manhood."

"Oh, well, good. You know how much I respect your work."

Our third-floor suite—yes, I said suite—had a large sitting room and two bedrooms, each with its own bath. The rooms followed the theme of the reception hall, formal with high ceilings, marble floors, and huge windows across the front.

I lined my bags up on the floor, pulled out my notebook, and flipped to my Possible Problems list. Under *Hala Tarek*, I wrote *Helena Bendix* and then *Lord Dysart?* The question mark was because I wasn't sure about him. He seemed pretty harmless, but it was hard to tell. I wondered what Cass thought of him.

Cass pulled back the heavy damask drapes and flung open the French doors leading onto a balcony. "Let in some glorious late-afternoon Theban air and sunlight."

"I'm confused. You said Thebes. Aren't we in Luxor?"

"Thebes was the ancient name when Hatshepsut ruled. Arabs changed the name to Luxor when they overran the kingdom, long after her death. I think of the city as Thebes."

The balcony had views of the manicured garden in front of the hotel, a marina, and the Nile. Across the river we could see a line of green trees, and beyond them, the brown hills encircling the Valley of the Kings.

Cass stepped out on the balcony and lit a cigarette. She turned as an afterthought and offered me one. "Do you smoke?"

I went to stand next to her. "No."

"Good for you."

We leaned on the wrought iron railing and watched small boats with sails shaped like giant birds' wings cut silently through the water. The setting sun reflected pink off the white canvas. "Those sailboats are beautiful."

"Those are called feluccas. They are passed down from father to son for generations."

As the sun touched the tops of the hills, I had the disorienting feeling of being transported back to the time the city was called Thebes. Cass' profile with her equine nose and dark hair could have been painted in the tomb murals I saw in the library books. I shook my head to clear it and chalked the weird illusion up to jet lag.

Cass draped her arm across my shoulders. The pressure of her embrace felt great. She pointed toward the sunset. "Look, Ra is sailing his royal barge into the underworld." She took a deep breath. "I could stand here all evening, but we'd better get moving. Don't want to keep Dr. Tarek waiting. She holds our fate in her young and ambitious hands." She gave my shoulder a final squeeze and went into her bedroom.

The phone on the writing desk jangled. I hesitated answering. The call could only be for Cass, but I was her assistant, so..." Dr. Cassandra Stillwell's suite."

A man's voice with a British accent. "Miss Morgan, please."

Who in the world? "This is she."

"Miss Morgan, this is Arthur Timms, Dr. Bendix's assistant. Dr. Bendix suggested I call you. She thinks our meeting might be useful."

"She mentioned that."

"This is your first dig season in the Valley, I believe. It's my third. You're at Columbia?"

People's voices over the phone are funny. Sometimes they obscure the caller's true personality, and sometimes they reveal it. This guy came across as a real academic ass, British accent or no British accent.

"Yes on both counts." I didn't go into the fact this was my first dig season not just in the Valley but anywhere, and while I'd be starting Columbia in the fall, my creative writing studies would have nothing to do with Egyptology.

"I have some free time tomorrow. Shall we meet in the dining room for tea, at four o'clock?"

I wanted to check with Cass before agreeing to meet with him. I was suspicious about what Helena Bendix might be up to. "Let me consult with Dr. Stillwell's calendar and let you know."

"Of course. You may call me in Room Two-thirteen."

When I hung up, Cass was leaning against the jamb of the door to her bedroom with her arms folded. She had changed into a crème-colored silk blouse and slim black slacks. She looked great. "Bendix's assistant, right?"

"He wants to meet with me, he said, at her suggestion. Tomorrow for tea in the dining room. Should I go?"

"Yes. See what they're up to. Right now, you need to get a move on."

Chapter Seven

BY THE TIME WE got down to the lobby, Dr. Hala Tarek was waiting. So this was the dragon. As Alfi said, she was young, not much older than me. Mid-twenties, I guessed. Her black, curly hair was cut short. Her eyes were remarkable, the irises so dark you couldn't tell where they stopped, and the pupil started.

Cass ordered tea, and Dr. Tarek got right down to business. "Now, Dr. Stillwell, how can I help you?"

"I appreciate your coming all the way from Cairo to meet with us. We have applied to the Ministry for a dig permit. I suppose the paperwork is wending its way through your office."

"I've seen your application. You're still searching for Hatshepsut."

"Yes, and while the permit forms cover the dry facts, I appreciate the opportunity to add context for you directly and to answer any questions you have. Of course, we hope you can make a positive recommendation to the Minister."

Dr. Tarek tented her fingertips. "Dr. Stillwell, I've read your research, and I'm aware of the skepticism about your theories among the American and the UK academic communities. Your application doesn't indicate who is backing you, nor does it explain how your expedition will succeed this time."

"Our expedition is independent of the funding sources you mentioned. If you know my work, you're aware that my theories about Hatshepsut's true place in history are controversial. The consensus among traditionalists is that being female, she could only have been a regent for her minor stepson, Thutmose III. I believe she was King in her own right. As to our prospects for success, I have the benefit of new information."

A thrill ran up my back. I was about to find out what Cass was carrying around in her locked briefcase.

Dr. Tarek leaned forward. "What new information?"

Cass' hand, usually so steady, trembled as she sipped her tea. "Dr. Tarek, I want to be as forthcoming as possible, but if this information were to fall into the wrong hands...I know you of all people understand how valuable finding Hatshepsut would be. She could make careers and fortunes."

The dragon settled back in her chair. "Which one are you after, the academic recognition or the money?"

"Neither. I don't want the wrong people to find her and take her away to a museum in New York or London or, heaven forbid, some ego-driven private collection where the truth about her place in history might be lost forever."

I pictured Lord Dysart beaming, standing beside a brightly colored pharaoh's coffin in his family's ancestral home in England.

Tarek looked out the window toward the marina. The river was impossibly calm. The boats tied up to the dock were so still they looked like a painting. "Hatshepsut belongs to the Egyptian people. With all due respect, if you were truly so concerned about keeping her safe, would you be trying so hard to bring her forth to be poked and prodded by foreigners? The people of my country deserve that our heritage is protected."

Cass leaned forward. "But don't the people of the world deserve the truth about her accomplishments as a woman?"

"Dr. Stillwell, do you know how many of the Egyptologists applying for dig permits in our country are Egyptian? Five percent. For almost two hundred years, since Napoleon rode around the desert in his funny hat and tight pants, foreigners have been looting our heritage. To you outsiders, our treasures might appear limitless. They are not. Do you know Napoleon's army burned mummies as fuel in their campfires? Did they teach you that at Oxford?"

I held my breath and waited for an angry reaction from Cass. Tarek was being unfair, holding Cass responsible for the sins of past generations. She practically accused her of being a tomb raider. Cass' lips were a tight, hard line. "You are a scientist, Dr. Tarek, and I suspect you trust only the evidence you observe. I may be foolish to try and convince you to trust me on my word. But I will find Hatshepsut, with or without your help."

I had a very bad feeling the encounter with the Ministry representative might end right there. I could practically hear my gran saying, 'Don't cut off your nose to spite your face.'

I raised my hand, like I was in class. "Wait!" The word came out way too loud. "You two have some common goals. Couldn't you consider how you might help each other? If you don't trust words, maybe you can sign a written agreement. Dr. Stillwell would share her new evidence and promise not to take our discoveries out of Egypt. Dr. Tarek would agree to keep Dr. Stillwell's evidence confidential and to support our permit application."

Silence. I held my breath and looked from one to the other. Tarek settled back in her seat, which I took as a hopeful sign. "First, I need to understand this new information making you so confident about finding her. We've had enough of hordes digging random holes in the Valley of the Kings. Of course I would guarantee confidentiality."

Cass hesitated and sipped her tea again. "I have proof Senenmut moved Hatshepsut from her original tomb, to save her from Thutmose III, and he left clues to her final resting place."

"I've read your theories. How do I know this is different? What proof do you have?"

"If we sign an agreement, I will share my proof with you." Cass folded her napkin. "Shall we meet again in Suite Three-oh-one tomorrow morning, say at eleven?"

Tarek gazed out the window at the boats again, silently considering the possibility of trusting Cass. She was making a mental pros and cons list, something I would have done. On the plus side, Cass might have some legitimate new clues to finding Hatshepsut. On the other hand, Cass might be just another posh British academic looking to make a name for herself.

I held my breath.

"We can meet."

After Dr. Tarek said goodnight, we headed for the elevator. The doors closed, and Cass grabbed me by the shoulders. "Brilliant! I knew you were the one for me. Levelheaded. Eleanor told me, and she was right. You saved the day." She pulled me to her and kissed me full on the mouth. "Of course, there are details we have to work out. I must have full control of the dig and the analysis of what we find..."

I could hear her talking, but I couldn't make out the words. What did the kiss mean? People don't go around kissing each other on the lips, do they? Was she merely feeling an abundance of exuberance, or did the kiss invite something more? The elevator stopped on the third floor, and Cass led the way down the hall, still chattering about a potential agreement with Dr. Tarek. Should I kiss her back?

While I carried on an internal debate, Cass opened the door to the suite and gasped, "Oh, no!"

She jerked me inside and slammed the door. All the drawers from the writing desk were pulled out and scattered around the room, their contents dumped on the floor. Cass' brown leather briefcase lay face down under the coffee table. She knelt beside the table and turned the case over. It was ruined. Someone sliced through the leather strap holding the lock.

"Who did it?"

"Someone left-handed."

"How do you know that?"

Cass laid the case face up on the coffee table and took a letter opener from the desk to demonstrate. She held the letter opener in her left hand. "Assume I'm left-handed." She slid the flat of the blade under the ruined strap. "If I'm in a rush to get into the case, I make an upward slash with the knife, cutting through the strap from left to right. The cut didn't manage to go all the way through, so the thief, being a bit sloppy and a lot in a hurry, tore it the last half inch or so. Therefore, left-handed. Interesting fact. Only ten percent of the world's population is left-handed. More men than women."

She turned the case upside down and shook it. Empty. She ran into her bedroom and came out holding what looked like a rolled-up piece of old fabric. "Thank heavens. He took the crystal and my notes but left behind the papyrus. Lucky I was studying it before we went downstairs to meet Tarek. He wanted to make things look like a robbery and was in too big a hurry to be very thorough about it. He must have known where we were and how soon we'd be back. He went straight for the case." She sat on the sofa and blew out a big breath.

"Papyrus? Crystal? I don't get it."

"They are the keys to finding Hatshepsut."

"I hope you'll tell me what you mean by the keys, but right now shouldn't we call the police or someone?" I looked around the ransacked room. "At least the hotel management."

"No, no! They're likely to tie things up. Don't say anything to anyone. Once the thief reads my notes, he'll be back for the papyrus. We can catch him in the act."

"He left the papyrus, but what did you say about a crystal?"

"It's a long story. Let's sit on the balcony."

A gentle breeze blew from the Valley of the Kings, across the Nile, and ruffled a wisp of dark hair that escaped her ponytail. "I happened on the clues to finding Hatshepsut two years ago, with the help of Howard Carter and Herbert Winlock."

"Wait, weren't they archaeologists who died fifty years ago?"

She nodded. "To understand, you need to know about two early-twentieth-century discoveries. Seventy years ago, a young British Egyptologist, Howard Carter, undertook clearing the oldest royal burial site in the Valley, thought to be the tomb of both Hatshepsut and her father, Thutmose I."

I wanted to interrupt and ask the spelling of the unfamiliar name. In my notes the name came out *Titmouse.* The expression on her face stopped me asking. Her look was the same as the first time I saw her in the Met in front of the statue of Hatshepsut, as though she heard voices from the past.

"Carter dug for three years in this one tomb before he finally reached the burial chamber, only to find her gone. Her sarcophagus was there, but it was empty. Carter assumed, along with the rest of the academic establishment, that her stepson and successor, Thutmose III, had destroyed her mummy, just as he tried to erase all the evidence of the powerful female ruler by chiseling away images of her as King on the temples and monuments she built.

"Carter resealed the tomb and moved on to other projects. He became obsessed with finding a relatively obscure boy-king, Tutankhamun. Twenty years later, he found him, an event that overtook his whole life and career. He never went back to Hatshepsut's tomb. After ten years excavating Tutankhamen's treasures, Howard Carter retired from fieldwork and spent his time lecturing about finding Tutankhamen. In fact, I've read you could often find him here in the lobby of this very hotel, holding court for anyone who wanted to hear the story of his first glimpse of the treasures of the boy-king."

I nodded. "I've heard the story about when he first opened Tut's tomb. Someone asked, 'Can you see anything?' and Carter answered, 'Wonderful things.'"

"Yes, imagine how he must have felt." Cass pushed up from her chair. "I could use a brandy. How about you? You don't smoke, but do you drink?"

"I'll try one."

She handed me a glass of mahogany-colored liquid and settled back in her chair. "The second discovery you need to know about happened around the same time Carter saw Tutankhamen's 'wonderful things,' twenty years after he found Hatshepsut's empty tomb. An American working for the Met, Herbert Winlock, made a remarkable discovery in the shadow of Hatshepsut's funerary temple. He uncovered the unfinished tomb of Senenmut, Hatshepsut's trusted advisor. Winlock found no mummy or funerary furnishings, just shards of broken pottery and rubble left by the artisans who stopped working in the middle of completing the tomb.

"Like Carter, Winlock was disappointed by an empty tomb, but one day, toward the end of the dig, a water boy stumbled on a remarkable find. In a niche, tucked away in the very back of the burial chamber, was a small rosewood chest, sealed with Hatshepsut's cartouche."

K-A-R-T-O-O-S-H? I'd have to look the word up later.

"Winlock decided to leave the seal unbroken and the chest unopened until his next trip back to New York. He pictured staging a dramatic reveal to impress the powers that be and donors at the Met. But things didn't work out as he planned. The American stock market crash in 1929 and the resulting Great Depression dried up financial support for the Met's Egyptian expeditions. The museum called Winlock home to New York. He served in two or three administrative positions with the museum and became Museum Director in 1932. Hard financial times continued for the institution. He would have had his hands full just keeping the doors open. The rosewood chest remained in his private collection."

Cass finished off her brandy. I had barely touched mine, which was for the best. My head buzzed and my tongue felt thick from the few sips I had taken. "At some point he opened the chest, right? And how did you get it?"

"I told you this is a story of two discoveries, the one by Carter of Hatshepsut's empty tomb and the one by Winlock of the chest in Senenmut's unfinished tomb. There's a third discovery that brings the two together. A month ago, I discovered the chest with the keys to finding Hatshepsut."

I was taking notes furiously, which made the story hard to follow. I decided to get the words down in the moment and study the story later.

"Winlock died in 1950 and left his papers, including his extensive journals, to the Met. A month ago, I was rereading his journals, for probably the fiftieth time. I sometimes read them when I get down in the dumps. I've been feeling quite morose for the past two years. Not myself."

What was she down in the dumps about? I mentally checked out for a moment to fantasize holding her in my arms and comforting her. Two years ago would have been around the time her last article was published and she got a bunch of bad critiques, including Bendix's "pulp fiction" comment. What a bitch!

Cass went on with her story. "In one of Winlock's journals from the late 1930s, I happened upon an entry I had missed before. Winlock described a dinner he and his old friend Howard Carter shared in

Winlock's home in New York. It was only a few months before Carter's death. He was in New York to deliver a lecture about Tutankhamen.

"Winlock confided his plans to retire from the museum and return to Luxor for a last dig. He showed Carter the rosewood chest and its contents, a papyrus and an ancient crystal. Winlock describes a pleasant evening, the two old colleagues poring over the text and debating its meaning. It's hard to say whether Carter encouraged or discouraged Winlock's plans. Maybe there was a little professional jealousy on Carter's part. Whatever, Winlock never made the trip. He retired to Florida where he died, leaving his estate, including his private collection of antiquities, to his only son. When his son died, he left everything to his son, Winlock's grandson.

"A month ago, after I read the journal entry, I tracked the grandson down in Florida and flew there. He's a lovely man, a stockbroker, interested only in the immediate future and its impact on the stock market, not in the ancient past. The rosewood chest was sitting on a bookshelf in his study. I told him how important the contents might be to answering some confounding questions about the most powerful woman in history. His grandfather might have answered them if conditions and times had been different. When he heard the story, the grandson was happy to sell the chest and its contents to me."

"What does the papyrus say?"

"It's in Senenmut's hand. Here, I'll show you." She led me to the desk and bent over to turn on the lamp. The gold charm on her necklace dangled in her cleavage. She caught me staring and smiled. She leaned forward and placed her finger behind the charm and lifted it. "It's Hatshepsut's cartouche. A gift a while ago from someone very special. It often pulls me out of the doldrums."

A gift from who? I wanted to ask, but the time wasn't right.

She carefully unrolled the papyrus. It was covered with hieroglyphics. I could catch the meaning of some of the writing from my study of Egyptian Grammar on the plane trip. I read the symbols for Hatshepsut, Re, and Wepawet, the god who was supposed to lead souls through the underworld.

"This first part is Hatshepsut's *Book of the Dead*. It's the story of Hatshepsut's passage through the underworld to eternal life with Re. But that's not the unusual part. Here at the end, Senenmut wrote instructions on how to use the crystal to find Hatshepsut."

"A treasure map."

"Not exactly. Maps weren't common during Senenmut's time. It's more a step- by-step instruction manual about how to fit the crystal in exactly the right place at exactly the right time of day. When we do that, we'll find her at the end of a beam of light."

Cass moved the lamp closer to the papyrus. "This last part is a curse. It says, 'To him who disturbs this crystal with evil in his heart, death shall come on swift wings.'"

A shiver ran down my spine. I didn't usually believe in curses, but there was something about this one that seemed different. "Do you believe in the curse?"

"I believe precious ancient treasures like the crystal should be protected from evil intent. Dr. Tarek and I agree on that score. If it takes a curse to do the trick, that's fine with me."

"Cass, you promised to meet with Dr. Tarek tomorrow to sign an agreement and show her the new information, which you don't have all of."

"I'll leave her a message at the desk that I'm feeling under the weather and put her off till the next day. If I'm right, once the thief reads my notes and gets finished kicking himself for leaving an important piece of the puzzle, he'll be back. We'll catch him in the act and recover the crystal and my notes."

The voices of a man and woman arguing drifted up from the garden below. Then the woman laughed loudly. The laugh wasn't mirthful, more harsh and mocking. We went onto the balcony and looked over the edge. Directly beneath, Helena Bendix and Lord Dysart faced each other on the walkway, their noses not more than six inches apart. Suddenly, things got physical. She reared back and socked him hard on the right cheek. He stumbled backward, holding the spot where she hit him. He lunged at her, took hold of her scarab necklace, jerked it from her neck, and stalked away. Bendix stamped her foot and ran back toward the front door of the hotel.

"Wow! What was that about?"

"Obviously there's more between them than Helena let on. I suppose it's none of our affair."

Cass went to the desk and rolled up a sheaf of hotel stationery and placed it in the briefcase. "There, that'll be the bait. I'll go down and get Sam to put the real papyrus in the hotel safe."

Chapter Eight

I SLEPT TILL NOON the next day. Jet lag.

I found Cass sitting on the balcony, facing the river. The smoke from her cigarette rose in a straight ribbon in the still, heavy air. "There's coffee. It's Egyptian. You may find it too strong and sweet, but many people develop a taste for it. You can order some American if you'd rather."

I poured a cup of the thick, fragrant liquid. It smelled great, and actually didn't taste bad at all. Not bitter as I'd expected. You almost wanted to chew it instead of drinking it. I grabbed my notebook from the desk and sat down beside her on the balcony. "Sorry I slept so late." I opened my notebook and found the next blank page. "What's on our agenda for today?"

"I'm afraid I'm in one of my moods." She fiddled with her gold necklace. "I can't stop thinking about what Dr. Tarek said, about bringing Hatshepsut out in the open to be poked and prodded by foreigners."

I thought it was a little late for a crisis of conscience, after we'd traveled halfway around the world.

"Leave me alone for a while." She turned to face me. "Sorry, that sounded harsh. I need some quiet time to think about the break-in and our next move. My brain stores away details in my subconscious. There might be some information to help us get the crystal back, and I need to focus without distractions in order to analyze."

It did strike me as a little harsh, but I couldn't say she didn't warn me. "No problem. I'll catch up on my notes from yesterday then write my mother and gran a letter. Maybe I'll walk down to Karnak Temple. Stretching my legs will feel good."

"Good idea. Take a hat." Cass was back to contemplating what was stored in her mind.

I grabbed my sunhat, notebook, a pamphlet called "Inside Luxor" off the desk, and my Egyptian Grammar. Might as well practice deciphering the hieroglyphics in the temple. I found an unoccupied writing desk in the lobby and composed a quick letter to Mother and Gran, putting in lots of details about the plane trip and our ride through the Sahara Desert to the hotel. I left out the parts about driving on the wrong side of the road and about getting robbed.

I expected Karnak Temple to be like a church where people came to worship their ideas of gods. Instead, the pamphlet said ancient Egyptians believed the temple was the actual home of whatever god the reigning pharaoh favored. In Hatshepsut's case, Amun-Re. People weren't allowed inside, only the pharaoh and a few priests.

Thirty-five hundred years later, on this hot July day, hundreds of tourists circulated through a forest of massive stone columns shaped like lotus plants. They followed their guides in clumps, gawking at the carvings of pharaohs making offerings to gods. If this was once the house of Amun-Re, he moved out a long time ago.

I stepped to the side of the hall, out of the flow of traffic, and opened my notebook to sketch some of the carvings. A man rushed past me and bumped into my arm, sending my notebook flying.

"Sorry, luv." He tossed the words over his shoulder, not even turning to look at me and certainly not making any move to pick up the book. He was English, from the accent, and dressed in starched khaki pants and shirt with a bright yellow kerchief around his neck.

I retrieved my book and considered chasing after him to give him a piece of my mind. He rushed to a corner of the hall and shook hands with a Middle Eastern guy in a dark suit, the same one who had stared at me in the hotel lobby yesterday. The dark suit guy gave the khaki guy one of those handshakes where the one guy holds the other's elbow. Sort of an intimate dominance thing. They spoke for a moment, then went out through the back area of the temple.

I wandered through the entire temple complex and ran back to the hotel in time for my tea date with Bendix's assistant, Arthur Timms. The dining room was full of people in groups and a few singles too old to be him. In the middle of the room, Dr. Helena Bendix sat at a table across from Dr. Hala Tarek. Bendix was doing all the talking, gesturing toward the hills beyond the river. I took a seat two tables away from Bendix and Tarek, close enough to overhear their conversation without being obvious.

Waiters in scarlet tunics floated among the white tablecloths serving high tea, tiny butter sandwiches with one little piece of parsley and pastel-colored cubes of cake, about an inch wide. I would definitely need some supper later. I opened my Egyptian Grammar. Might as well study until he showed up.

"Miss Morgan from America." He didn't phrase it as a question, but a self-confident statement. I looked up from my book into the face of the rude guy who bumped into me at the temple. Up close, I could see he was late twenties, tall and thin with slicked-down hair. My gran said never trust a man with slicked-down hair. His starched and spotless khaki pants and shirt and yellow kerchief looked like the movie version of clothes a person might wear digging in the Sahara Desert. Arthur Timms gave the impression of never kneeling in the sand with a trowel and never sweating. He gave no indication he recognized me from the temple.

"Arthur Timms?"

"I am." He looked me up and down, taking in my limp shirt and pants and dusty boots, and sat across the table.

I glanced over at Helena Bendix. "Listen, if you need to be with your boss, meeting with Dr. Tarek, we can reschedule, no problem." I crossed my fingers, hoping he'd take me up on the offer.

"Oh, no." He dragged his response out sarcastically. "That meeting is far too important for a mere graduate assistant. There might be credit due, if she's successful. My job is to keep my mouth shut and write every single word of every single paper she puts her name on."

Had Timms written the "pulp fiction novel" comment? Bastard!

He snapped his fingers to signal a waiter. "And in the meantime, I'm supposed to act as her glorified secretary, opening and answering all her mail. Don't tell me the fabulous Dr. Stillwell is any different."

"Yes, she is."

"Maybe now but wait till the honeymoon is over."

What an idiot. He didn't know me. Why would he say these things to me? A loud bang made me jump. Bendix had stood up so abruptly that she knocked her chair over backward. She leaned across the table and shook her finger in Dr. Tarek's face.

"You listen to me, young Miss Holier-Than-Thou. Our permit is already approved by your superior, the Minister of Antiquities. I don't know what your game is. Maybe you want a payoff of your own. Whatever, you and he better get your act together." Helena stormed out of the dining room.

Two waiters rushed over to the table. One righted the chair, and the other asked if he could get anything for the woman left sitting at the table. Dr. Tarek shook her head and shooed them away. She sat for a few moments looking at her hands in her lap. She folded her napkin, stood up, her spine as straight as a poker, and left the dining room.

I looked at Timms with my mouth hanging open.

He smiled and shook his head. "Oh, dear. Looks like there won't be any credit coming out of this one."

I got through with Timms as fast as I could. I only half listened to him switching between bragging about his own academic achievements and complaining about Bendix. Half-listening was plenty for him, as long as I nodded and said "Mmm" every so often. I hoped he would bring the dark suit guy from the temple into the conversation, but he was totally consumed with academic politics. I squirmed in my seat, anxious to get back with Cass and tell her about what just happened between Bendix and Tarek. I worried the argument might affect our deal with Dr. Tarek.

As soon as I could get away, I ran across the lobby to the elevator and jabbed the call button several times. The car didn't come, so I took the stairs two at a time to the third floor. I burst into the suite and almost tripped over Cass on her hands and knees in the middle of the sitting room floor. She held a flashlight in one hand and tweezers in the other. "Careful!"

I froze. "What is it?"

She held up the tweezers. "A clue. It's a tiny bush okra seed. Assuming our carpet was cleaned before we moved in..." She tapped her lip. "We need to check that with housekeeping. Put a follow-up item on your list."

She was clearly excited about her find, and it seemed like her bad mood had lifted. I grabbed my notebook. While I was at it, I flipped to the Possible Problems list and added *Arthur Timms* and *Dark Suit Guy*.

Cass sat cross-legged and inspected the seed. "Anyway, assume the carpet was cleaned. Bush okra seeds have been used for thousands of years, even until today, as a thickener in soups and stews. It's sold in the market. You and I haven't walked in the market, so our intruder may have brought the seed in on his shoes."

I wrote it all down, but it seemed a real stretch that a bush okra seed could help us get the crystal back.

I sat on the floor beside her. "Cass, I have to tell you what happened. There may be a big problem with Dr. Tarek." I described the confrontation in the dining room between Dr. Tarek and Bendix.

"And after Bendix stormed out, tell me very specifically what happened."

I closed my eyes and replayed the scene in my mind. "Well, Bendix had knocked over her chair, and a waiter rushed over to pick it up. Another one hustled to Tarek's side to see if she wanted more tea or anything. She shooed them away. She sat with her head down for a while, I would say two or three minutes, then slowly and deliberately folded her napkin. She got up and walked out without looking right or left or speaking with anyone. I felt for her. There were lots of people in the dining room, and you couldn't help hearing the whole thing. She must have been so embarrassed."

"From your description of her reaction, I'd say both embarrassed and furious. Helena hasn't been having a very good two days. First the fight with Dysart in the garden and now this." She patted my knee and left her hand there. "Excellent description, by the way."

Was I supposed to read this intimate gesture as an invitation? The timing didn't seem right. It also seemed like I was spending a lot of time trying to interpret Cass' intentions. Should I just come right out and make a pass at her?

Cass stood up and took an empty envelope from the desk and dropped the seed in.

Too late. "Aren't you worried Tarek will take a disagreement with Bendix out on us, too? What should we do now?"

"First things first. Tonight, we catch a thief."

Chapter Nine

LIGHT FROM THE FULL moon, shining through large windows in Cass' bedroom, made a pattern of squares on the carpet. Like the bars in a jail cell. I felt a nervous chill. We had been sitting on the floor in the dark for about an hour. Cass was sure the thief would be back. I wasn't so sure. Wouldn't he assume Cass was smarter than to place the papyrus in the ruined case and leave it in the desk?

"Cass, won't the thief assume you've hidden the papyrus in a safe place?"

"Never underestimate the self-centeredness of a crook. They always believe everything will go their way. They're like compulsive gamblers and politicians in that regard."

"And never trust a man with slicked-back hair."

"What?"

"Just one of my grandmother's sayings. Arthur Timms has slicked-back hair."

Cass shifted her position, and I saw a metallic glint under her leg. "Is that a gun?" The situation seemed serious before, but things just got a lot more serious. "Is a gun a good idea? Do you know how to use it? I shot a deer rifle at a buck once, but I missed. Of course, I missed on purpose, but still...and I certainly don't know anything about a handgun. Where did you get a gun anyway?"

"Calm down. Alfi got it for me, and it's not loaded. It's just to scare the thief."

"What if he has a gun, too?"

"Then our gun will even the odds."

As I opened my mouth to object again, she shushed me. I heard the scratch of a key in the keyhole outside the hallway door and the creak of hinges you don't notice until you're sitting in a dark room, holding your breath, about to confront a burglar.

Cass put her finger to her lips again and crept to the bedroom door to peep through the keyhole into the sitting room. She pantomimed "One person with a flashlight." Slow scraping sounds as he opened each desk drawer. The front door hinges creaked again, and then a surprised shout, "Hey!" Then a sickening hollow crack and heavy thud and the slam of the front door.

Cass scrambled to her feet, threw the bedroom door open, and flipped the light switch. Helena Bendix lay on the Persian carpet.

Funny the details that imprint on your mind. The first thing that struck me was how still she was. It was a different stillness than someone merely asleep, deeper and more permanent. Even though I had never seen anybody dead, I knew right away she was definitely dead. She was face up with her right leg bent under her body at an awkward angle and her arms thrown out. She looked like she was inviting a hug. In her right hand, she held a flashlight still turned on, casting a washed-out beam of light against the wall. Beyond her left hand, the ruined briefcase lay with blank pages of hotel stationery spilling out.

Her hair formed a frizzy orange halo around her head, and underneath it a pool of dark red was creeping across the rug. But the most awful part was the expression on her face. Her eyes were wide open, and her lips formed an "Oh!" Her brain had an instant to register surprise that she was being murdered. *Death will come on swift wings.* Senenmut's curse!

A stone figure of the god Horus, with the head of a falcon and the body of a man, lay beside her. The small statue usually sat on our mantel. I leaned over to pick it up.

Cass grabbed my wrist. "Don't touch that."

I pointed at the body. "It's Helena Bendix." Okay, that was completely unnecessary. I was sort of in shock.

"Yes, I suspected she was the thief."

"How did you know?"

"Of everyone here, she would stand to gain the most from finding Hatshepsut. She'd be willing to take the risk. Also, she's left-handed."

Left-handed? I got a picture of Bendix in the garden slugging Lord Dysart...with her left hand.

"Remember the slice on the leather strap of my briefcase, when the crystal was stolen, went from left to right."

She lifted the telephone receiver and dialed the front desk.

***

Samut Paneb, the hotel's Evening Manager, stood at attention in a corner of our sitting room. He looked absolutely miserable. Imagine somebody being murdered in your fancy hotel. In the room of a famous archaeologist. And the famous archaeologist was someone you really admired. Miserable.

I was biting a hangnail and answering the uniformed policeman's routine questions–name on passport, country of origin, date of arrival in Luxor, and purpose of the trip. The man in charge, Detective Inspector Salem, Luxor Police, wore a grey suit and wrinkled white shirt with a tie that looked like he knotted it in the dark. He circled the body, making notes on a small pad. It reminded me I was absent-mindedly carrying my notebook around. I turned to the Possible Problems list and marked through Helena Bendix's name.

The detective kept glancing at Cass, leaning against the desk with her arms folded. He knelt and inspected the left side of Bendix's head, where she took the blow. He looked up at Cass and pointed to the figure of Horus on the floor beside the body. "The murder weapon. Is it yours?"

"The hotel's. It was sitting on the mantel. How do you know it's the murder weapon?"

The detective didn't respond but kept making notes. Was he annoyed, or did he dismiss a female "civilian" opinion? Too bad. He would be way ahead if he included Cass in the investigation, and Cass would get the crystal back more quickly. She had already labeled him incompetent, and she wasn't making any bones about it. My gran always said, 'You can catch more flies with honey than vinegar.' As a kid, when I heard her say that I would picture a bowl of honey covered with flies. Why would anybody want flies in their honey?

"So it was here when you checked in?"

Cass nodded.

He looked up; his pencil poised over his notes. "That is a yes?"

"Yes."

"And you know the deceased?" He glanced at his notes. "Professor Helena Bendix."

Cass stuffed her fists in her pockets. "Detective Inspector, my assistant and I are happy to answer your questions, but someplace other than in this room." She glanced at Helena's body. "Dr. Bendix's death is very upsetting for both of us."

The detective gestured with his pencil toward Sam. "Mr. Paneb has been assigned to work with us on behalf of the hotel. I'm sure he will relocate your belongings as soon as we've completed a thorough search of your rooms."

Sam stepped forward and nodded to Cass.

Salem bent over the body again. "I'll be asking you and all the other guests to gather in the dining room. Mr. Paneb, please have your staff notify them. I'm assuming most will be in their rooms and asleep at this hour. And I will need everyone's passport. The guests will remain inside the hotel for at least the next forty-eight hours while we conduct interviews and thorough searches of all the rooms."

Chapter Ten

CASS AND I WERE the first hotel guests in the dining room. We took a small table at the back and watched the others drift in, most in robes, pajamas, and slippers, and a few stragglers who had taken the time to dress. Cass focused like a laser on each of the thirty or so people and appeared to take mental snapshots one by one. A low, nervous hum grew as people passed around the news of a murder in the hotel. Sam circulated through the room, supervising waiters pouring coffee and tea. He still looked miserable.

I thought about my mother and gran sitting in the kitchen in North Carolina. I could picture my next letter: *Dear Mom, Luxor is very interesting, and I'm a suspect in a murder investigation.*

Cass read my mind again and patted my hand. "Don't worry. We'll be fine."

Hala Tarek came through the entrance and paused under the archway. She looked composed and wide-awake. I peeked around Cass to see if Tarek would show some indication of how she was feeling about us. She might even come and sit with us, which would be a great sign. Sam hurried over and escorted her to a seat in the middle of the room.

Lord Dysart and Arthur Timms came in. Dysart was dressed in his usual white linen suit, but instead of his customary crisp, starched look, his clothes were rumpled. His eyes were red-rimmed. Lack of sleep or grief? Or guilt? He took a seat near the front of the room. Timms sat across the table from him. He was dressed in a white ankle-length cotton dress and sandals, the kind I noticed Egyptian men wearing in the street market we drove through when we first arrived in Luxor. Timms, with his thin frame, pasty skin, and slicked-down hair, looked ridiculous in the traditional dress. Like he was going to a costume party.

Dark Suit Guy was the last to come in. He looked neither left nor right, went straight to the back of the room and found a seat.

"Cass, don't look, but do you know who that man is?"

She turned around in her chair.

"I said don't look! Do you know who he is?"

"No, why?"

"He's got some connection with Arthur Timms."

Detective Inspector Salem strode into the room, as if someone had given him a cue. There couldn't have been more of a difference between the swarthy, unkempt policeman and the small crowd of entitled, white, and mostly elderly Americans and Europeans. He made no effort to put anyone at ease. "There has been a murder in the hotel where you are staying."

The low murmuring started again.

"My men have begun searching each of your rooms…"

The murmuring turned into out-loud objections from some of the men. "I say, sir, are you allowed to do that without our permission?"

"By what right are you searching our rooms?"

A woman said, "Someone call the British Consulate."

"And the American," another voice said.

The detective glared around the room until the group fell silent again. "I assure you, your consulates have been notified. You will remain in the hotel for at least the next forty-eight hours. I will be holding your passports. Mr. Paneb will accommodate all your needs. As we complete searching your rooms, you will be allowed back in them." He turned and left.

"This is outrageous." A large man with a flushed face scraped his chair away from the table and stood up. "My wife and I, and I think others in the room, are embarking on a cruise of the Eternal Nile in a few hours." He said Eternal Nile not in a reverent way, but almost sneering. "And it's not cheap, either. Why, we could practically buy a whole boat on one of our rivers back home for what we're paying. We don't even know this woman they say's been murdered. Never met her. Somebody needs to do something. What about you?" He pointed at Dysart. "Aren't you a lord or something?"

Lord Dysart opened his mouth to reply but thought better of it.

The man's wife put a restraining hand on his arm. "Harold, he's an earl."

He jerked his arm away. "Whatever."

Cass cleared her throat. "How many of you have travel plans in the next two days?"

About half the group raised their hands.

"Mr. Paneb, can you speak with the Detective Inspector about starting the room searches with these guests? Perhaps they could be cleared to carry on with their plans."

The angry man sat down. "That's more like it. Finally, somebody making some damn sense."

Sam gave Cass a look that said, *Thank you so much for defusing the situation.* He rushed off to find the policeman. Waiters and kitchen staff began laying out white linen tablecloths on a breakfast buffet table. Smart move. At least the guests would have full stomachs.

Cass leaned over and whispered, "If we're to recover our crystal, we've got to find the killer in the next forty-eight hours. We can't trust Detective Inspector Salem to get that done."

"But how are we going to do it? We're suspects!"

"I'm not sure yet how we'll do it. I just know we have to."

"Where did you hide the gun? Aren't you worried the cops will find it when they search our room?"

"That's the least of my concerns right now. The gun wasn't fired, and Helena wasn't shot."

A uniformed policeman came into the dining room, looked over the group, and consulted a piece of paper in his hand. He called the names of the angry man and his wife. "Follow me, please."

For the next five hours, the officer collected the Nile River tourists, two by two. The tourists didn't come back to the dining room, so apparently Cass' suggestion worked. Their rooms had been searched, and they were questioned and cleared by Detective Inspector Salem to experience the Eternal Nile. Sam relaxed a little as the crowd thinned out. He circulated around the room, chatting with the rest of us and directing the waiters to keep coffee and tea coming. When Sam approached us with a refill, Cass silently slid my notebook toward him. She didn't want the cop getting his hands on my notes. Sam took it without a word.

"Miss Ariadne Morgan." The uniformed policeman motioned toward the door. They were getting down to questioning those of us who knew Bendix, and the move probably signaled they had finished searching our suite. I looked at Cass, and she gave me an encouraging smile. She knew I was a truth teller. Maybe she was concerned I'd give away too much. I was concerned about that myself. I remembered Perry Mason counseled his client, "Answer the direct question and don't add anything."

I followed the policeman to the elevator, and we went up to the third floor. I hoped I wouldn't have to see the dead body again, and I felt more than a little relieved when he led me across the hall from the murder scene to a different suite.

They had moved the writing desk to the middle of the room and placed a straight-backed chair in front of it. The suspect chair. The windows of the suite faced away from the river to the east, and the sun was just rising over the jumbled streets of the city in the background and the Temple of Luxor below. Traffic was already building up, autos and motor scooters racing around the obelisk in the middle of the square where we were when I first glimpsed the Nile and the Valley of the Kings. Could that have been only two days ago? The policeman motioned toward the chair and took up a position behind me.

Sam came in with a tray of coffee and water and set it on the coffee table. He served me a cup and gave me a little encouraging look, which made me feel a bit more at ease.

Right on cue again, Detective Inspector Salem came out of one of the bedrooms, wiping his hands on the front of his pants, and sat behind the desk. He had my passport and his little notebook in front of him. He opened the passport and took up his pencil. "Ariadne Morgan. Am I pronouncing the name correctly? English names are sometimes difficult."

"That's correct."

"You are twenty-three years old." That wasn't a question, so I waited for him to go on.

"Your passport was issued very recently. The journey to Luxor is your first international trip with these credentials?"

My first international trip, period. "Yes." I saw another TV show where they administered a lie detector test, and the tech first asked some easy questions to calibrate his machine. I suspected Salem was calibrating his internal lie detector.

"Where do you reside, Miss Morgan?"

Now that was a hard one. I didn't live at Barnard since I moved out of the dorm. I didn't live at Columbia yet, and I hadn't felt I lived in North Carolina since high school. I picked one. "Beaufort, North Carolina...America."

"What is your relationship to Dr. Cassandra Stillwell?"

"She's my employer."

"How long have you worked for Dr. Stillwell?"

"Three weeks."

Salem stopped writing. "Only three weeks?"

"Yes." I could hardly believe myself that only a few days before I was sitting on the Columbia campus across from Eleanor, drinking coffee and leering at her boobs.

"Were you acquainted with the victim, Dr. Bendix?"

"I met her for the first time two days ago, here in the hotel."

He nodded and made a note in his book. "Tell me about events in your suite last night."

Open-ended question, the hardest for me because I wouldn't know when to shut up. I decided to answer like making a list, mentally ticking events off one by one in my head. "We suspected a burglar might break into our rooms. We waited in the dark in the bedroom, to try and catch him in the act. Just after midnight, the burglar opened the door with a key and started searching through the desk. Another person, the killer I guess, came in the front door. I heard four sounds: a shout, a crack, a thud, and the slamming of the front door. We found Dr. Bendix dead on the floor. We called hotel management, and they called you."

I held my breath and waited for his follow-up questions, like "What made you think a burglar would enter your room?" and "What were they after?" and "What's missing?"

Instead, he asked, "Do you own a pistol, Miss Morgan?"

He had found Cass' gun. "No." That was technically true. Not my gun.

Salem pushed his chair a little away from the desk and lit a cigarette. He consulted his notes. "Thank you, Miss Morgan. Mr. Paneb has relocated you to a suite down the hall. The officer will show you." He held up a brass key on a fob.

That was it? "I can go?"

"You're free to go anywhere on the hotel property." He put my passport in his suit coat pocket.

We passed the door of the murder scene as a technician with a black medical bag in his hand came out. Was she still lying on the floor in there? Would they close her eyes after they took all the photos and fingerprints?

Our suite was at the end of the hall. The key made a scratching sound as I searched for the keyhole, the same sound Bendix made when she broke in our room. Hey, how did Bendix get a key to our suite? While I was pondering that question, I made a quick survey of our new rooms. Sam had moved us seamlessly, unpacking and putting things away, including my Egyptian Grammar on the coffee table and my toothbrush in the toothbrush holder in the bathroom. My notebook lay in the middle of the bed.

I grabbed the grammar book and my notebook and sprinted down the back stairs, across the lobby, and into the dining room. Cass was waiting for me. Dr. Tarek sat at a table alone. Lord Dysart stood motionless in front of the large front window with his hands in his pockets, staring across the river toward the west bank. Arthur Timms joked in Arabic with one of the waiters, a darkly handsome, very young man. Dark Suit Guy was drinking coffee and reading a newspaper.

Cass motioned me over. "It appears Salem has narrowed the prime suspects down to the six of us. As long as Detective Inspector Salem is correct, that the killer is in this little group, we'll get our crystal back, and he'll solve his murder case. For now, we need to let him go through his process. Tell me about your interview."

I recounted the questioning word for word, including the part about the gun. "It means he found your pistol, right?"

"I didn't try to hide the gun. She wasn't shot, and the truth is we had a gun only to defend ourselves. Did Salem ask you what the thief was after?"

"No. I told you every word of what he asked me. I was waiting for that question and a lot of others, but he just let me go."

"He'll come back at you. He's just getting started. But we'll know who the killer is by the time that happens." Cass stared over my left shoulder and whispered, "Here comes something."

I heard someone behind me clear his throat. "Dr. Stillwell, please excuse me if I'm interrupting, but I couldn't pass up this opportunity to introduce myself." It was Dark Suit Guy.

He bowed from the waist. "Napoleon Hassan."

Cass nodded. "Please join us, Mr. Hassan. This is my assistant, Miss Morgan."

"Charmed." He bowed in my direction and pulled out a chair. He straightened the cuffs of his white shirt and touched the cufflinks, small green glass scarab beetles set in gold that matched the larger one on Helena Bendix's necklace. "Dr. Stillwell, I am an ardent follower of your theories and your search for Hatshepsut. I myself am a curator of very rare antiquities."

"A dealer."

"If you prefer. I like to think I connect discerning clients with very special artifacts that educate the world about the glorious history of the Egyptian people."

"Quite." Cass traced the rose embroidered on the white tablecloth with her fingernail. "Mr. Hassan, it appears that those of us in this room are connected somehow with Dr. Helena Bendix. How did you know her?"

"Your late colleague and I both appreciate...in her case, appreciated...the value of rare, beautiful things. She occasionally introduced me to persons of her acquaintance who shared that appreciation."

"Potential buyers."

Hassan cleared his throat again. "Yes."

"And you paid her a commission."

"Yes. She provided a valuable service for all parties involved. I was more than happy to compensate her for it."

"I see. Well, since you are familiar with my work, you know that my interests lie more with discovering insights about the people in ancient cultures than with the material artifacts." Cass extended her hand. "As a matter of fact, my assistant and I were taking this opportunity to get some work done. I hope you'll excuse us if we get back to it."

Hassan jumped up from his chair. "Of course, of course. I've intruded on you too long. Forgive me. Dr. Stillwell. Miss Morgan." He bowed to each of us and hurried back to his chair in the corner.

"Ugh! What a slimebucket. I feel like I need a shower."

"Yes. A prime example of the kind of opportunist Hala abhors."

"I've seen him twice before. The day we checked in, in the lobby, he stared at me oddly. And I told you he has some connection with Arthur Timms. Yesterday, when I went to Karnak Temple, they were over in a dark corner getting very chummy."

"Interesting." She patted my hand. "Let's go talk to Sam about room keys and how someone might have gotten into our suite."

Exactly my question. I quickly turned to my Possible Problems list and added a name: *Napoleon Hassan.*

Sam was at his usual station behind the registration desk. "There are only three keys to your suite. Each of you was given one upon your check-in, and there is a spare in my office, in case something were to happen to yours."

"Is the spare still there?"

"Come with me." Sam opened a door behind the registration desk and motioned us into a tiny office with a desk, two chairs, and a massive safe that looked like one Butch Cassidy and the Sundance Kid dynamited. On the wall behind the desk was a pegboard with spare room keys. 301 was hanging there.

Cass nodded. "Are there master keys?"

"Yes, I have a master." He pulled a key attached to a gold chain from the watch pocket in his vest. "And the maids have masters for the guest rooms. I'll call the head housekeeper. She may be able to shed some light on this."

Sam picked up the phone, spoke in Arabic, and almost as soon as he hung up, there was a knock on the door. Sam opened it for a short lady, as round as she was tall. She wore a crisply starched grey uniform and carried a clipboard. She made a little bow to Sam and said something in Arabic. I got only two words: "Syd Paneb." Mr. Paneb, in English.

"Mrs. Bennu, this is Dr. Stillwell and Miss Morgan. Please speak English."

She made a little bow to each of us. "I am sorry, Syd Paneb, for my delay in coming. We are shorthanded today."

"No matter, Mrs. Bennu. Have you had any reports of master keys going missing?"

Her hand flew to her heart. "Oh, no, sir!"

"We need to speak with the maid assigned to three-oh-one day before yesterday."

Mrs. Bennu checked her clipboard. "That was Nia, but Syd Paneb, she has left sick today. She is why we are shorthanded. She arrived at work on time, at five o'clock this morning, but the news of the English lady was so upsetting to her that she had to go home. It's very unlike her, Syd Paneb. She is a most dedicated worker."

"Thank you, Mrs. Bennu. I'll let you get back to your work." He patted her hand. "Don't worry. This will all sort itself out."

After the door closed, Sam took a thick ledger from his desk drawer. "I have Nia's address here."

"Good. I'll ask Alfi to go to her house and talk to her about the key. Sam, do you have occasion to be in the room when Detective Inspector Salem questions people?"

"I serve coffee and water in the suite where the interrogations happen. Perhaps I could linger out of the way and overhear some of the questions."

"That would be helpful."

Chapter Eleven

WHEN WE GOT BACK to the dining room, Dr. Tarek was gathering up her papers to follow the uniformed policeman. Dysart was still standing at the window.

"Let's see what Lord Dysart has to say for himself."

Cass walked over to him, and they exchanged a few words. The two of them headed toward the lobby. Behind his back, Cass beckoned me to follow them.

We found two stone benches across from each other in the garden, hidden from view behind a hedge. Dysart sat on one, crossing his legs at the knees. Cass and I sat opposite him. "Lord Dysart, this is a terrible ordeal for all of us, but especially for you. I understand what her death means for your expedition."

"Excuse my appearance." He smoothed the lapels of his linen suit and gingerly touched a bruise on his right cheekbone. He must have gotten it when Helena slugged him in the garden. "Yes, this is all bloody inconvenient."

Inconvenient? That sounded cold for someone whose colleague—maybe more than a colleague—had been murdered.

"My role with the expedition was to come along and help with obtaining our dig permit. For my influence with the Minister of Antiquities. Totally aboveboard, of course. And I'm financing the entire expedition. With this development, I'll have to reevaluate. I assume Columbia or the Metropolitan Museum of Art is funding your work this summer?"

"No, I'm working independently for now."

"Ah, so you're funding your Hatshepsut dig yourself."

Cass nodded.

He stroked his mustache. "Do you have any idea when we may be released?"

"I'm afraid we're the primary suspects in Helena's murder right now. The Detective Inspector isn't likely to let any of us go ahead with our plans. Ari has been questioned already, and I suspect he may call her in again. He's with Dr. Tarek now. You, Mr. Timms, Mr. Hassan, and I will follow."

"Bloody inconvenient."

"May I ask how you came to be working with Dr. Bendix?"

"About a year ago, she read a description of our collection of New Kingdom antiquities and wrote to me asking permission to study it." He looked down at his lapels and tried to smooth the wrinkles again. "We often get these requests, of course. I think Helena mentioned to you we've managed to amass a collection that rivals any in private hands, or many museums, for that matter."

"Helena did mention your collection, and you must be very proud."

"Yes. Well, Helena began traveling regularly from Oxford to our home, Hammond House in Richmond. I was impressed with her academic credentials and her passion. Over time, we developed a strong collegial connection." He emphasized the collegial part. "My wife is not well, you see. We have no children, and with the estate practically running itself, I have time to indulge in what others might call my hobby. It's more than a hobby for me. It's a passion." That passion word again. "I know you of all people understand the allure of owning these precious artifacts."

"My interest has always been in the people, not the things."

"Quite so."

The uniformed policeman appeared around the hedge. "Lord Dysart. Come with me, please."

"Of course, my good man. Lead the way. The sooner we get this done, the better."

I turned to the next blank page in my notebook and began taking down the conversation with Dysart. "Did you see the bruise on his cheek from Helena slugging him? He could have killed her, couldn't he? Do you think he did it?"

"If so, he's very cagey. Too soon to tell. What he said about influencing the Minister of Antiquities was interesting. It was important to him we do not suspect he was offering bribes, something Helena implied in her argument with Tarek. Dysart is another perfect example of what Dr. Tarek deplores, a foreigner plundering the history of her people. Can't say I disagree with her."

"He seemed on the verge of offering to finance your dig."

"Yes. That's not ever going to happen." Cass stood and brushed her skirt. "We've missed lunch. Let's order some early dinner in the room, then find Tarek."

The elevator doors slid open on the third floor. There was a uniformed policeman leaning against the doorframe of the murder suite, smoking. Across the hall, the door to the interrogation suite was closed.

Cass led the way down the hall and stood aside for me to unlock the door. I swung it open, and the toe of my boot caught the edge of a white envelope and sent it skittering across the rug.

Cass knelt to pick up the envelope. "Hotel stationery with my name typewritten on the front." She opened it and unfolded a single sheet of plain white paper with typewritten text. She read it aloud.

My dear Dr. Stillwell,

By now it is clear you and I are at an impasse. I have the crystal and you have the instructions on how to use it to find our beloved Hatshepsut.

I trust you are not depending on Detective Inspector Salem for a solution. He has neither the resources nor the wits. We'll all be released in a few hours, and a proposal suggests itself—might not you and I join forces? An English expression comes to mind: "Half a loaf is better than none."

I may not be the partner you would choose, all other things being equal, but I am your only hope at this point. If it makes the prospect more palatable, while Dr. Bendix was clearly a reprehensible human being, I did not mean for her to die. There was an urgent need for action. She already had the crystal. I simply wanted to prevent her getting her hands on the papyrus. What followed was a regrettable accident.

Please give my proposal your consideration. I will be back in contact soon.

"No signature, I'm sure."

Cass folded the letter and put it back in the envelope. "No, but this is excellent. We're on the road now."

"I don't see how."

"He, or she, is feeling the same time pressure we are, and if we're careful he'll show his hand first. Also, I suspect he's a classic narcissist. They're easily identifiable if you know what to look for."

"Wait." I ran and grabbed my notebook. "Ready."

She ticked the characteristics off on her fingers. "First, they deflect responsibility and blame the victim. Everything is always someone else's fault. You can see that in the letter. He claims he didn't mean her to die. Second, they have a grandiose view of their own importance. Others could not survive without them. Also, in the letter. He says he's my only hope. Third, they use people to make themselves look more successful financially, professionally, academically, or culturally."

"Timms!"

"Yes, or Dysart, or Hassan, or maybe even Tarek."

It seemed to me we needed to start eliminating suspects pretty soon or we'd run out of time. Maybe Cass was already doing that without telling me. "What do we do next?"

Cass went to the telephone. "I'm going to call Alfi and see if he's found the maid, and also ask him to check his sources and find out if someone is enlisting excavation workers. The Detective Inspector is running out of time. As soon as he releases us to leave the hotel, it's likely the killer will start preliminary efforts to get a dig organized."

She talked to Alfi, then hung up the phone. "He found Nia. He'll come here tomorrow to give us the details, and he'll check on anyone doing dig preparations. Now, let's find Dr. Tarek and tell her about the crystal and the papyrus."

"But what if she's the killer?"

"If she is, she already knows about them. If she isn't, we might be able to enlist her as an ally."

Her room was on two, one floor below, so we took the back stairs. A used room service tray on the floor outside her door made my stomach growl. In our excitement about the letter, we had forgotten to order dinner.

Cass knocked.

"Yes?"

"Dr. Tarek, it's Cass Stillwell and Ari Morgan."

She opened the door with the chain on. "Yes?"

Cass stepped where she could be seen clearly from inside. "I hope we're not disturbing you. These have been a chaotic few hours. Are you willing to carry on with the discussion about our excavation application?"

Tarek hesitated a second before taking off the chain and let us in. Her room looked like ours, except not a suite. There was a bed in what would have been our sitting room. She was on the same side of the hotel as us, with a view west across the river. The chair at her writing desk was pulled out and the lamp illuminated a paper, half covered in writing. She held an ink pen in her left hand, the kind you fill with actual ink, and her fingers were stained with it. No typewriter in sight.

Tarek put the pen and paper in the desk drawer and turned off the desk light. "We can sit on the balcony. I'm afraid I have only water to offer you."

"We're fine, thank you." Cass sat down and leaned toward Tarek with her elbows on her knees. "I want to share with you the new information I have about Hatshepsut's resting place. I hope this information will convince you to support our efforts."

Cass skipped the background story of Carter's early excavation of Hatshepsut's empty tomb and his discovery twenty years later of King Tut's tomb. Tarek knew all of that. Cass told the story of her discovery of Winlock's journal notes describing his New York dinner with Carter and of the rosewood chest and its contents.

As the story went on, Tarek leaned closer and her breathing speeded up. When Cass got to the part about finding the chest in Florida and buying it from Winlock's grandson, Tarek interrupted. "You have proof in Senenmut's hand that he moved Hatshepsut, and you possess the clues he left for how to find her."

"There are two clues. I have one, the papyrus. Dr. Bendix's killer has the crystal and my notes. I plan to get them back."

Tarek stood abruptly and leaned against the balcony railing. "I must ask you to stop now."

"Why? Surely you see the importance of what I'm telling you."

"That's why you need to stop. You see, Dr. Stillwell, I can't help you."

"What do you mean?"

Tarek turned her back to us and stared across the river for a moment. "I'm going to trust you. I hope I'm not being foolish doing so." She walked inside to her desk, took a piece of paper from the drawer, and handed it to Cass. It was typed on hotel stationery, like the one someone slid under our door.

My dear Dr. Tarek,

Your Minister of Antiquities has made a commitment, in exchange for a significant sum of money, to approve certain activity in search of important archaeological finds. You are personally standing in the way of that commitment. We have a saying in my country, "For every promise, there is a price to pay."

You will not like the price you have to pay if you continue to block us.

Tarek turned to me. "Miss Morgan, you were in the dining room. You heard Dr. Bendix intimate the Minister of Antiquities, my superior, has taken a bribe."

"I heard it. You couldn't miss it."

Tarek sat down across from Cass again. "I was trying to sort out what to do when someone slipped that under my door. My duty is clear. I'm writing to the Prime Minister recommending we suspend all expeditions until this gets sorted out. One of two things will happen: either I'll be believed, and the Prime Minister will suspend digs, or I will be fired. In either case, I can't help you."

Cass folded the letter and handed it back to Tarek. "There's a third possibility. Whoever wrote this letter might carry out his threat. You must be careful. This letter may have been written by Helena Bendix's killer."

"My duty is clear."

Cass shook her head. "I admire your principles, and I'm not suggesting you compromise them. You might choose, however, to let things play out a bit longer before you bring the Prime Minister into the matter. If Detective Inspector Salem finds Dr. Bendix's killer, you'll have evidence about who tried to compromise the approval process. You can present the Prime Minister with a complete picture."

Cass took my elbow, drew me up, and steered me toward the door. "Whatever you decide, I urge you to be careful."

Tarek closed the door behind us, and we heard the scrape as she put the chain back on.

"Think she'll take your advice to let things play out?"

"Maybe. You saw how excited she was about the prospect of finding Hatshepsut."

"At least we can cross her off the list of suspects."

Cass shook her head. "Not yet. She may have sent the letter to herself. I'll bet you're starving. I know I am. Let's get some supper and turn in early tonight and get an early start tomorrow morning. Half of our forty-eight hours will be gone by then."

Chapter Twelve

THE NEXT MORNING WE went down for breakfast. Our footsteps on the marble mosaic floor echoed off the walls. The lobby was empty except for Sam behind the registration desk, and Arthur Timms marching back and forth in front of the desk. Cass put a restraining hand on my arm.

"This is unspeakable." Timms's face was bright red. "I'm a British citizen, and I demand to know by what right I'm being detained in this hotel." He lifted his right hand to consult his watch. "I have important business to conduct."

Sam folded his hands behind his back and stood up even straighter, if that was possible. "These decisions are in the hands of the Detective Inspector, sir. I can look up the telephone number of your consulate here in Luxor, if that would be useful."

Timms turned away and brushed past us toward the stairs. He almost ran headfirst into a uniformed policeman coming down.

"Mr. Timms, come with me, please."

Timms followed him, muttering under his breath.

Cass and I went up to the desk. "Hello, Sam."

"Dr. Stillwell, my apologies for the scene." He straightened his ascot with a shaky hand and glanced around the empty lobby. "I have information." He pulled a folded paper from his inside coat pocket. "I drew a picture as accurately as possible, given my limited time and artistic talent. The police found a necklace in Lord Dysart's room, hidden in his closet in a shoe."

I looked over Cass' shoulder. It was a sketch of the front and back of Helena Bendix's scarab necklace. The back had an engraving. *To My Flame-haired Goddess from your Worshiper. P.*

"When the Detective Inspector asked Lord Dysart about the necklace, he acknowledged that it was a gift to Dr. Bendix. The clasp was broken, and Lord Dysart said he was planning to get it repaired for Dr. Bendix, before her murder, of course. It was hidden in the shoe until he could have me put it in the safe."

"Good, Sam."

"There's more. Lord Dysart was very concerned that details of Dr. Bendix's murder be kept confidential. He repeated several times that his wife isn't well and that the embarrassment of anything sordid would upset her and her family. Apparently, the family fortune is all from her side."

"Thank you, Sam. Mr. Timms is being questioned now. Can you listen in?"

"I'll try."

Just then Alfi came in the front door, and Sam seated us in the dining room before hurrying away with a tray of coffee and water for the police.

Cass and Alfi ordered Egyptian coffee, and I joined them. I was developing a taste, just as Cass predicted.

She took a sip and turned to Alfi. "You found the maid."

"Yes. She stays with her sister in the Nubian sector. They are from Aswan and the family was relocated to Luxor when the new dam flooded their village."

"Does she know anything about the key?"

"She does, but she's very afraid to talk about what happened because of the English lady's death. She was crying the whole time I questioned her. She said two days ago, in the afternoon, the red-haired lady and a man found her cleaning the suite across the hall from three-oh-one. The lady told her she accidently locked her key in her room and asked Nia to open the door to three-oh-one with her passkey. Nia was reluctant, since it's against the rules, but the lady got very angry and threatened to report her. Nia opened the door."

"I can picture Helena bullying her. What did Nia say about the man?"

"He stayed in the background. The only thing she would say is he looked English."

Cass clicked her tongue. "Too bad she wouldn't say more. Go on."

"Nia always kept her passkey attached to her cleaning cart. Yesterday, when she came to work early in the morning, she noticed the passkey was missing altogether. She was working up the courage to tell the head housekeeper and risk losing her job when she heard of Dr. Bendix's murder. That's when she went home sick."

"Do you think she would say more about the man if the police questioned her?"

"Maybe, if they can find her. When I left her sister's house, I stopped just down the road. I watched Nia get into a rattle-trap truck parked in front of the house. She was carrying a bundle, probably all her earthly goods. I suspect she's on the road back to Aswan."

"That's bad luck."

"Yes, but here's some better news. I do have some information from my source about an Englishman organizing workers for a dig in the Valley of the Queens."

Cass embraced Alfi. "You are the best!" I felt a definite twinge of jealousy.

"How did you find out so fast?"

"My brother, Ebo, is an agent. The Englishman approached him about recruiting twenty-five workers."

"Who is the Englishman?"

"Arthur Timms."

Sam appeared in the archway and gestured to Cass. She folded her napkin. "Finish your breakfast. I'll be right back."

In a few minutes, Cass came back holding a piece of paper. "Sam copied this off a crumpled letter the police found in the waste bin in Timms' room." She placed the copy on the table in front of us.

Helena Bendix
Associate Professor of Egyptology
Queen's College, Oxford
C/O The Winter Palace Hotel
Luxor, Egypt

My dear Dr. Bendix:

I received your wire of 21 June 1972, requesting "immediate authorization" to terminate the assistantship of Arthur Timms. While you, as supervisor in the field, have wide discretion as to Mr. Timms's status, I hardly need to point out how impactful such a move would be for Mr. Timms's career. I assume you have considered all options before suggesting an extreme action.

Still, I would appreciate a fuller discussion of the basis for your recommendation before we agree on a next step. I understand both the urgency of your request and the need for discretion. Perhaps we could arrange a telephone call, at your convenience, of course.

Very truly yours,
James Carnes
Professor of Egyptology
Queen's College, Oxford

Cass folded the paper and put it in her pocket. "How do you suppose Bendix's letter got into Timms's room?"

I raised my hand again, like I was in class. "I know! Timms told me one of his duties was opening all of Dr. Bendix's mail. He intercepted the letter. She never saw it. She should have been more careful."

"Indeed."

"He killed her because she was trying to fire him."

"Maybe, but we need to know more. Why was she trying to fire him? The head of her department at Oxford was clearly reluctant to take precipitous action." Cass shook her head. "Save me from academic politics."

Chapter Thirteen

THE LOBBY WAS EMPTY except for Cass and me and Mr. Hassan. He was smoking a cigar and reading the newspaper, which seemed like the thing he did most of the time. I wrote my mother and gran another letter, avoiding the bizarre situation we were in and trying to make things sound normal.

"Do you think the police will call you last?"

"Appears that way. The only other person left is Hassan."

"Dr. Cassandra Stillwell." We both jumped. The uniformed cop was back.

Cass winked at me and rose to follow him. "Wait for me here, keep your eyes open for any activity by our friends." She nodded toward Hassan. "And don't worry."

Cass trailed the cop to the elevator.

Familiar throat-clearing sounds. "Miss Morgan." It was Hassan. "I wonder if you would do me the honor of joining me for lunch."

I checked my watch. "I'm short of time right now."

"A cup of coffee, then."

Cass said keep my eyes open, so this seemed like a good way to do that. "Okay."

Hassan picked a table near the window that faced the marina. "The river is restless today. I'm afraid our ancient country isn't showing itself to its best advantage for your visit."

He made me sound like a tourist. "I'm lucky to be working with Dr. Stillwell, whatever the circumstances."

"Certainly. Mr. Timms tells me this is your first dig in the Valley of the Kings."

"Yes."

He waited for our server to bring our coffee, then he leaned in conspiratorially. "Dr. Stillwell made it very clear that she is unavailable to participate in the commerce that is so important for the Egyptian economy. I wonder if you feel the same. Your financial circumstances are, I suspect, much different from hers."

"What do you mean, exactly?"

"The antiquities trade has two sides, demand and supply. Dr. Bendix and I worked together on the demand side. She introduced me to wealthy individuals who wanted to own treasures from our past. Mr. Timms and I collaborate on the supply side. He is in a position to alert me to interesting finds from the expeditions that you Americans and British turn up. I suspect that you soon will be in the same position."

So that's what Timms and Hassan were meeting about in Karnak Temple. "Is that legal?"

"That is a difficult question to answer in black-and-white terms. You'll forgive me an observation about you Americans. You tend to lurch from absolute to absolute. We Egyptians prefer to keep things more fluid and open to interpretation."

I thought about something Gran said, but decided I'd better keep this bit of wisdom to myself. 'Anybody who goes down the middle of the road is bound to get run over.'

Hassan fiddled with his shirt cuffs. "I'll answer you this way. As far as our government is concerned, if the sale and ownership is to individuals interested in scientific study in an archaeological context, it is legal. Which all my buyers certainly are. Of course, there are some highly placed individuals, such as our current Prime Minister, who hold a more radical point of view."

I remembered our first meeting with Dr. Tarek. I was pretty sure she would take one look at this guy and call him a crook. I pushed my chair back. "Please excuse me, Mr. Hassan. I promised to meet Dr. Stillwell in the lobby."

He stood up and held out a business card. "Take my card. You may reconsider."

***

Cass was gone for two hours. I wrote the whole encounter with Hassan in my notebook, then tried studying hieroglyphics, but it was impossible to concentrate. Finally, she came out of the elevator, walked across the marble mosaic floor, and collapsed into a chair next to me. She blew out a big breath.

I slammed the book shut. "What took so long? What did he ask you?"

"All the questions we thought he'd ask you. Why were we staked out in the bedroom waiting for a thief? Why did I have a gun and where did I get it? Why didn't I report the theft of the crystal the day before? All expected. Something unexpected was that he had a copy of the *American Journal of Archaeology* in which Helena was critical of my work."

"How did he get that?"

"Timms gave it to him."

That weasel! It made Cass look like she had a motive for killing Bendix.

"Did you tell him about the papyrus and the crystal?"

"Yes, but not the whole story. He knows they're precious artifacts, but he doesn't know about finding Hatshepsut. He wanted to confiscate the papyrus, but I talked him into leaving it in Sam's keeping in the hotel safe."

"Why would he agree to that?"

"By the end of my interview, he was beginning to see I might help him solve the crime. The Governor of Luxor is under enormous pressure from the British to find the murderer, and the pressure passes down the line and lands on Salem. The forty-eight hours run out tomorrow at dawn. If he doesn't come up with an arrest, the Egyptian National Police are likely to step in and take the investigation out of his hands."

Cass leaned her head back against the leather lounge chair and closed her eyes.

"Are you all right?"

"Yes." She opened her eyes and smiled. "Don't worry. It's not a mood coming on. I think the events of the last two days are catching up with me. Let's go upstairs and sit on our balcony."

As we passed the front desk, Sam called to Cass. "Dr. Stillwell, you have a letter." He handed a long white envelope across the desk.

Cass showed me the typewritten address on the front: *Dr. Cassandra Stillwell.* "How did you get this, Sam?"

He motioned toward the rows of mail slots behind the desk, one for each room number. "Someone left it in your box. He must have put it there when I stepped into my office for a moment."

We took the stairs to our suite and sat side by side on the balcony facing the river. Unlike other days since we arrived, a stiff wind agitated the water into whitecaps. The boats tied up in the small marina bobbed on the ends of their tethers like corks. The path that ran along the edge of the water was deserted in the heat of mid-day.

Cass tore the letter open.

My dear Dr. Stillwell,

The Bard's Richard II moaned, "I wasted time and now doth time waste me." Or as your very charming southern American assistant might put it, "Time's a-wastin'." As I suspected he would, Detective Inspector has run out of time. He appears no closer to a solution than when he began. You and I will soon be free to follow the clues Senenmut left for the resting place of Hatshepsut.

I have the crystal and your notes. While I'm sure the search would be more efficiently carried out with Senenmut's own words as a guide, I'm willing to proceed without the papyrus. You see, I'm actually doing you a favor by offering a collaboration. And while Dr. Bendix is beyond any personal benefit from the outcome, I believe even she would see the wisdom of my proposal.

We are likely to be freed tomorrow morning to leave the hotel grounds. If you would like to discuss this further, meet me at 10 in the morning by Hatshepsut's fallen obelisk at Karnak Temple.

Cass folded the letter and put it back in the envelope.

I felt a shiver of fear that we might be in over our heads. This person was truly evil. "Shouldn't we tell the Detective Inspector about these letters, Cass? We may be in real danger."

Cass patted my hand. "We don't want to spook the killer and scare him off. He's ready to show himself. Don't worry, we'll be fine."

I pulled Hassan's business card from my pocket and handed it to Cass. "I have news, too. Mr. Hassan made me a proposition. He offered to pay me for stealing artifacts from digs. He has the same deal with Timms. That's what they were talking about when I saw them in Karnak Temple."

Cass took the card. "What did he say, exactly?"

"Just a minute." I grabbed my notebook and read her the conversation, including the slur against Americans and his justification for why black-marketing antiquities was perfectly legal. "This takes him out of being a suspect in Bendix's murder, doesn't it? He was making money off her. Why would he kill her?"

"Maybe, or maybe not. There could have been a business deal gone bad."

The phone rang, and Cass jumped to answer it.

"Yes. Yes. Do you know why?" She hung up. "It was Sam. Detective Inspector Salem wants us all in the dining room right away."

***

There were about a dozen people seated in the dining room when we arrived, including Dr. Tarek, Arthur Timms, Lord Dysart, and Mr. Hassan. Salem came strolling in after we were all settled. A guy who looked like he meant business came in behind him. He was dressed in a white cotton bush jacket and matching pants with a black beret and a pistol on his hip. He stood at attention behind Salem, but not in a deferential way. It was more like he was observing Salem to evaluate how on top of the situation the detective was.

Salem had neatened up the knot in his tie, but he still looked like a mess. There were dark circles under his eyes, I figured from lack of sleep. He glanced at the guy behind him and turned back to us. "In the last two days, we have made progress with our investigation. However, it is a very complex situation. There is certain forensic evidence being processed. We expect the matter will be resolved soon." He gestured toward the beret guy. "This is Major Hakim with the Egyptian National Police, who has been assigned by the Governor's office to assist with the investigation."

The guy in the beret stepped forward. "Ladies and gentlemen. We appreciate your patience with this inquiry so far. You are valued guests in our city, as was Dr. Bendix, and your safety is very important to us. The Governor asked me to extend his thanks as well." This guy was a lot slicker than Salem.

He took a piece of paper from the inside pocket of his jacket and read a list of names—the remaining hotel guests besides Dysart, Timms, Tarek, Hassan, and the two of us. "If I have read your name, you are free to go. Please leave your contact information while in Egypt with hotel management. The Governor thanks you again for your patience and cooperation. If you plan to extend your stay in our ancient city, please enjoy yourselves."

He waited for the group to file out of the room. "Lord Dysart, Dr. Tarek, Dr. Stillwell, Mr. Timms, Mr. Hassan, and Miss Morgan, as Detective Inspector Salem says, we have made progress and expect the matter will be resolved soon. While you will be free to leave the hotel tomorrow morning, we're requesting you remain in Luxor until further notice. If you choose to extend your stay here at the Winter Palace, hotel management has promised to continue to keep you very comfortable. We will communicate regularly." He gestured to Salem, and they left the room.

Lord Dysart jumped up and followed the two policemen. "Major Hakim, a moment please."

Timms looked at Cass. "Outrageous! They have no right. Buffoons. Now we have not only the bumbling Inspector Clouseau, but they've added a military martinet to the equation. I'll be going to the British

Consulate first thing in the morning." He shoved back from the table. "You're welcome to come with me."

When Cass didn't respond, Timms huffed and stomped out of the room.

While I was trying to figure out if Beret Guy's appearance on the scene was good news for us, Dr. Tarek pulled out a chair next to Cass. "I've given much thought to your advice about my plan to send a letter to the Prime Minister. I'm afraid I share Mr. Timms's pessimism about the authorities solving Dr. Bendix's murder. I've decided to contact the Prime Minister."

Some small movement outside the entrance to the dining room caught my attention. By the time I focused, whatever or whoever it was had disappeared.

Chapter Fourteen

THE NEXT MORNING, THE ten o'clock sun, high in a cloudless sky, baked the stones paving the entrance to Karnak Temple. Tourists were gathering with their guides in groups sorted by the languages they spoke–Chinese, Japanese, Spanish, English, and others I couldn't guess.

Cass and I passed through the ranks of stone columns in the great hall and into the courtyard where Hatshepsut's obelisk lay on its side, toppled over centuries before. Time had obscured whether Hatshepsut's stepson, Thutmose III, deliberately pulled the monument down or whether it just fell over one day. I tried to imagine the sound the collapse would have made crashing to the ground, and how the average Egyptian, fishing on the river or plowing behind a donkey in his field, might have stopped and looked toward the temple in wonderment.

Cass and I slowly circled the obelisk. She pointed out carved figures and hieroglyphics celebrating Hatshepsut's accomplishments as pharaoh–military victories, trade deals, and reverent processions in honor of the gods. I opened my notebook and began copying the carvings. I figured staying busy was better than obsessing over why we were really there, to rendezvous with Helena Bendix's murderer and try to get back the crystal. Cass seemed the opposite of nervous, as calm as the swans paddling in circles on a small pond beyond the courtyard.

At the pointed section that was the top when the enormous granite needle stood outside the temple, the god Amun recognized Hatshepsut as the ruler of the two kingdoms. She was bare to the waist, with the narrow hips, broad shoulders, and flat chest of a male. Amun placed his hand on her crown, signaling his blessing of her kingship.

"Cass, can I ask you a stupid question? Why are ancient Egyptians always painted side-wise?" As soon as I got the words out of my mouth, I felt like an ass. It was the kind of question a tourist would ask a guide. Stupid.

Cass traced the carving of Hatshepsut's face with her finger. "It wasn't only the Egyptians who painted people from the side, but pretty much every civilization with art. Assyrians, Etruscans, Greek. While even the most inexperienced artists today understand the concept of perspective and how to draw the human face and figure from all sides, including face-on, the technique had to be discovered, the same as any other technical advancement."

The look on my face must have given away my embarrassment. Cass laughed that sexy, deep-from-the-throat chuckle I first heard back in New York. She pulled me behind the obelisk, out of view of the crowds, and held me by both shoulders. "You are so darling." Then she kissed me full on the mouth. It was no accidental, abundance-of-exuberance kiss. This was what I'd been hoping for since she kissed me in the elevator. I pushed her against the granite obelisk and kissed her back.

"Mmm, that's nice. We'll have to revisit this when we can focus. Right now, we must watch for our killer. He may be showing up any minute."

I backed away reluctantly and waited for my breathing to return to normal. "It's almost ten thirty. Do you think he's coming?"

"No. He may have gotten scared off. Or maybe he's taking advantage of the fact we're away from the hotel for some other purpose."

"What purpose?"

"I don't know yet, but we need to head back as quickly as we can." She grabbed my hand and pulled me through the giant stone lotus columns in the great hall and into the street. She hailed one of the dinky three-wheeled taxis waiting at the curb, and the two of us squeezed into the tiny back seat. Cass told the driver, "Winter Palace." The car backfired, belched a cloud of black smoke, and lurched into the flow of traffic headed toward our hotel, a mile and a half south.

The car skidded to a stop in front of the hotel. Dr. Tarek was sitting alone on a stone bench in the front garden. Cass paid the driver and headed toward Tarek. "Good. We need to talk with her."

Tarek stood when we approached her. She shook her head. "It's happened. I wired the Prime Minister yesterday, and this morning his chief assistant telephoned. I've been 'relieved of duty.' Meaning fired."

Then things happened very fast. I heard clicking sounds through the tree leaves overhead, and a spray of gravel kicked up at our feet, followed by a second and third. Cass grabbed me with one hand and Dr. Tarek with the other and pulled us down in front of the bench. "Bullets!" She peeked over the bench toward the hotel. "The shots came from the roof. Ari, come with me. Hala, find Sam and tell him to get the police."

Cass and I ran through the lobby and up four flights of stairs to the door leading to the roof. I was in front, and when I grabbed the doorknob, Cass put her hand over mine and whispered, "Wait."

She turned the knob and pushed the door open a crack. It slammed in our faces, then jerked open again. Arthur Timms, carrying a rifle, launched his body at us, knocking us both backward. Cass fell down a few steps. I was able to keep my balance, and when Timms scrambled past Cass, I dived onto his back. His momentum and my weight threw him forward onto his stomach. The rifle flew out of his grip and clattered down the steps. I rode him like a toboggan down the stairs to the landing below and sat on him until Cass got to her feet.

Timms struggled to escape. "Get off me, you bitch!" His face made my stomach lurch. His nose pointed to the right instead of straight ahead, and it was gushing blood. He dragged himself to the wall, sat up, and took a handkerchief from his pocket to try and staunch the blood flow. "You broke my nose, you idiot."

Cass grabbed the rifle and pointed it at Timms. "Where's the crystal? You and Helena broke into our suite and stole it, and you murdered her for it."

Timms let out a barking laugh. "I may have considered killing Helena. Heaven knows I would have been justified. But someone else saved me the trouble. And I don't have your precious crystal. Yes, she made me help her steal it, but she kept it. She was the one obsessed with your fairy-tale speculations about Hatshepsut, not me. Hatshepsut." He waved the handkerchief as if to dismiss the idea and 3500 years of history. The bleeding had slowed, but his nose was already turning purple. "I came to Egypt this summer for a real dig with authentic evidence behind it. This discovery will be as big as Tutankhamen. Bigger even."

"What evidence?"

Timms looked from Cass to me to Cass again and lowered his voice. He couldn't resist bragging. "I have a map showing the location of Nefertiti's tomb in the Valley of the Queens."

"Go on."

"You may be familiar with an obscure British amateur, Robert Hay." He said "amateur" as though it left a bad taste in his mouth. "He spent several years in Egypt, starting in 1827, exploring tombs and sketching monuments and hieroglyphics. He left a forty-seven-volume set of unpublished books with his notes and drawings in the British Museum Library. I found the map in one of the volumes.

"I went to Dr. Bendix right away, of course, and she secured Lord Dysart's agreement to finance the expedition and applied for a dig permit. All was well and good until she double-crossed me. She tried to get me fired so she could take all the glory for herself. Typical."

The landing door flew open and slammed against the wall. Salem rushed through with Hala behind him. He pulled Timms to his feet, twisted his hands behind his back, and hooked him up in handcuffs. "You're under arrest for the attempted murder of Dr. Hala Tarek and the murder of Dr. Helena Bendix."

"What? No! No, no! I tell you, I had nothing to do with Bendix's murder, and I wasn't really trying to shoot Tarek. I just wanted to scare her. Murder? No, absolutely no."

Salem shoved Timms down the stairs, and we all clambered after him to the lobby, which bustled with new arrivals checking in after the police had lifted the lockdown. Everyone froze in place at the spectacle of Timms in handcuffs. Then Beret Guy, Major Hakim, came running in the front door with his pistol drawn, followed by two other uniformed cops. Salem found a vacant lounge chair and pushed Timms into it. "Under control, Major. We caught him red-handed. I'll take him to Headquarters." I looked for Cass' reaction. Salem didn't catch anyone red-handed. Cass and I caught Timms. She gave a little headshake signaling me to hold my tongue.

Major Hakim motioned Salem to the side. "A moment, Detective Inspector." The two policemen talked in low tones, Hakim pulling rank and Salem objecting. Salem lost the argument. Hakim holstered his pistol, pulled Timms to his feet, and pointed him toward the door. "I'll take it from here."

"Wait!" Timms struggled and shouted over his shoulder to no one in particular. "Call the British Consulate. This is a mistake." How could he hope anyone in this group would help him? I remembered Cass' description of a narcissist. It fit Timms.

Major Hakim led Timms out the door, put him in the back of a police car, and drove away.

Salem blew out a frustrated breath. He opened his little notebook and turned to Cass, Hala, and me. "Tell me what happened."

"Shall we sit in the dining room?" Cass led the way to a table. She described the gunshots, our dash up to the roof, and my takedown of Timms. She left out Timms's story of the map to Nefertiti's tomb. "It's time to show him the letter, Dr. Tarek."

Tarek took the folded piece of hotel stationery from her pocket and pushed it across the table to Salem. "Someone, apparently Timms, slid this under my door. He threatened me, and now he's carried through with it. If not for Dr. Stillwell's quick reaction, he would have shot me."

Salem read the letter, refolded it, and put it in his pocket. "I need to question him. Dr. Tarek, will you come with me to Headquarters to sign a statement?"

Cass and I watched them leave. "Do you believe Timms is telling the truth about Dr. Bendix?"

"I hope he is, because that means we still have a chance of getting the crystal back before the police get their hands on it."

Sam appeared in the archway. "Dr. Stillwell, I found this note in your mailbox."

"Thank you, Sam."

He bowed and started away. "Sam, Miss Morgan and I will be having dinner tonight in our suite." She glanced at me with a small teasing smile that gave me a tingle you-know-where.

"Can the chef manage a Chateaubriand and whatever wonderful fresh vegetables have come in from your locals today? And a bottle of Chateau Haut-Brion."

"Of course." Sam hurried off.

If she was trying to impress me, it was working.

She opened the note, not a typewritten letter, a handwritten scrawl on a piece of paper torn from a notebook. She read it aloud. "Meet me at the marina tomorrow morning at nine o'clock. Bring the papyrus."

Chapter Fifteen

SAM PERSONALLY SERVED THE special dinner Cass ordered. He set up our table on the balcony with snow-white linens, china with the hotel crest in gold leaf, and crystal glasses. He held Cass' chair and then mine and lit the candles with a flourish.

The vegetables from local vendors tasted fresh and flavorful. The meal started with an epic green salad with tomatoes the likes of which I hadn't tasted since the beauties my gran raised in North Carolina, and hers were so good she won a blue ribbon every year at the county fair. The Chateaubriand—as it turned out, a fancy name for a beef roast—was amazing.

Sam poured the last of the wine into our glasses and disappeared. When the sun fell below the hills, the temperature dropped. A chilly breeze made the candles flicker. Cass sipped her drink. "Are you okay finishing our wine out here? The view across the river is magical tonight."

"Of course. This dinner tasted awesome."

"I wanted it to be special. With all the unexpected things that have happened since we arrived in Luxor, you deserve a treat." She reached across the table and stroked the top of my hand. "This wasn't what you bargained for when you agreed to come with me, but I don't know what I would have done without you."

I flashed back to the day on the Columbia campus, only a few weeks ago, when Eleanor slid the paper with Cass' phone number across the table. At the time, I felt reluctant and suspicious of Eleanor's motives.

Cass read my mind again. "I'll be forever grateful to Eleanor for finding you for me. Speaking of Eleanor, do you mind if I ask about your relationship with her?"

"Great while it lasted. She's smart and sophisticated, and she was honest with me. It ran its course. And I'll be forever grateful to her, too, for recommending me to you."

"I'm glad."

I took a swig of wine for courage. "Can I ask you a question? Who is the special person who gave you the necklace?"

Cass scraped her chair back and stood at the balcony railing. "Jessie Finn Markham."

"I recognize the name. She was the first author on your papers when you were getting started, at the beginning of your career."

"Yes, she was my professor at Oxford and my mentor. Over time, the relationship deepened into a special thing that I can't really explain or put a name to. We weren't physical, though we came close a few times. She was married and felt a deep morality about being faithful to her husband, though heaven knows she was within her rights. He was serially unfaithful to her. But it was more complicated than that. When one of us was ready, the other shied away. Neither moved to seduce the other. I think we feared the relationship might change, that something might be lost." She reached for her wine glass.

"She taught me our profession is more than digging up pottery shards. She loved discovering the lives of the people in the sites we excavated and communicating archaeology in new ways, in writing and film, with creativity and empathy. She called it 'archaeological imagination.' She wanted to bring attention to the unity of the past and present, events in antiquity that make us what we are today."

"That's what you believe, too, about finding Hatshepsut."

"Yes, it is. I want to prove she ruled in her own right as Pharaoh, not a mere placeholder for her stepson until he matured. She overcame unimaginable cultural barriers put up against her gender, and she succeeded through competence, not by force or intrigue."

"Where is Jessie Finn Markham now?"

"She died two years ago, of breast cancer." Cass began to cry.

"Oh, no." I grabbed my dinner napkin, went to her side, and took her in my arms. She leaned her head on my shoulder and sobbed. I held her and patted her back, not sure what else to do.

She finally cried herself out. She took the napkin and wiped her face. "I'm sorry. I haven't been able to talk about her to anyone else. I have a lot of stored up grief."

"And regrets?"

"No, no regrets."

She took my face in her hands and kissed me. Her lips were soft and super warm, I figured from all the crying. Her mouth tasted of the wine, sweet and peppery. She closed my eyelids with her thumbs and kissed each one, then kissed my neck. I felt a whooshing rush of emotion, not exactly sexual arousal, but more like a release of anticipation. It was the buzz you hope you experience at least once in life. Like, "This is what it's supposed to feel like when it's special." I held on to her waist to keep from stumbling backward.

She searched my face. "Are you okay?"

I nodded, which was all I could manage at the time.

She led me into her bedroom, pulled back the covers, and guided me backward to sit on the bed.

"Wait." I pulled her down beside me and began unbuttoning her silk blouse. The moonlight shining through her window reflected off the gold necklace, then her cleavage, then the breasts I'd fantasized about. They were even better in person.

She pulled my cotton camp shirt out of my pants and over my head without unbuttoning it, stripped off my pants and her own, lay back on the bed, and pulled me on top of her. I had a fleeting moment of performance anxiety. What does she like? She read my hesitation and held my hand and showed me how to start. Things took care of themselves after that.

***

Except for my recent bout of jet lag, I've always been able to wake up without an alarm. In college, whatever I had coming up the next day percolated in my unconscious all night and got me up early. The morning I woke up in Cass' bed was different. If not for her lips on mine and the aroma of coffee, I might have slept all day. She wore a scarlet silk robe that parted to show her naked thigh when she stretched to set down a room service tray with coffee. She kissed me again, and I tried to pull her back into bed.

She laughed that sexy way and brushed my hair out of my eyes. "Tempting, but we're late getting started. We have to go down to the marina and recover Senenmut's crystal. You get dressed. I'm going to finish my coffee on the balcony and have a cigarette."

I took a quick shower, toweled my hair dry, pulled out a fresh set of khakis, and laced up my boots.

"Ari. Bring your young eyes here a minute." Cass was standing at the railing looking toward the marina. "Isn't that Mr. Hassan walking along the river with Major Hakim from the National Police?"

Sure enough. The black beret stood out against white felucca sails. "Yep. That's them. They sure look chummy."

"Yes, they do."

Chapter Sixteen

ROWS OF FELUCCAS ON either side of the pier nodded in unison against the wind blowing off the eastern desert. Cass held under her arm the ruined leather briefcase with the papyrus inside. She turned toward the front of the hotel and shaded her eyes. "It's Hala Tarek. She's coming our way."

"Cass, is she the one who wrote you the letters? Is she the killer?"

"I don't know. Let's see what she says."

Dr. Tarek crossed the street and came down the cement steps toward us. "I got your note."

Cass shook her head. "I didn't send you a note. I got a note, too, to meet at the marina."

We felt a jolt. A felucca bumped into the piling, and Lord Dysart climbed awkwardly over the edge of the boat onto the pier. "Ladies." He held out his hand and indicated we should climb on board. This didn't seem like a great idea. Somebody was a murderer with a motive to make sure we didn't spill the beans. I looked to Cass for a sign. She climbed into the boat, and Dr. Tarek and I followed.

"Meet Omar." Dysart pointed toward the small, dark man at the stern. "The soul of discretion, and he speaks no English." Dysart gestured to him to cast off and joined us at the front of the boat. Omar pushed us away from the pier. The sail billowed as it caught the wind. The tiller wasn't a normal one; it was a log painted white. Omar climbed onto it with his bare feet and steered by balancing and walking back and forth, leaving his hands free to manage the sail.

The surface of the river was choppy. Miniature whitecaps roiled the water and bounced the boat as if it were moving across a rutted gravel road. Dysart stood up unsteadily in the bow facing us. "Ladies, thank you for joining me this morning. I have a proposal for our mutual benefit. I hope you will find it attractive.

"Dr. Stillwell, you have, I suspect in the briefcase you are clutching, an ancient papyrus, one of the pieces of a puzzle to finding Hatshepsut. Dr. Tarek, you possess the power to approve such an expedition."

Cass and Hala exchanged a quick glance. Dysart was clueless about Hala having been fired and that she had lost the power to approve anything.

"And I have this." Dysart reached into his inside jacket pocket with his left hand and withdrew the crystal. He held it over his head, and the sun beamed through the glass and speckled the bottom of the boat with a hundred points of light. "I also have the funds to finance the search for her. So I see myself, I hope you won't find this immodest, as a potential senior partner for our enterprise." He put the crystal back in his pocket and looked from Cass to Hala. "Your thoughts?"

We all stared at him for a minute. Cass recovered first. "You are holding my property, Lord Dysart. My thought, as you put it, is you need to return it to me immediately." She started to move toward him.

Dysart took a handgun from his left pants pocket and pointed it at Cass. "Please keep your seat, Dr. Stillwell. I'm disappointed at your reaction, but I can't say surprised. You don't strike me as the most practical thinker. More of a dreamer." I felt a rush of adrenaline. The muzzle of the gun looked as big as a canon. I scanned the boat for something I could use to defend us. Cass sat down and put a restraining hand on my knee.

Dysart waved the gun around and pointed it at Hala. "As for the crystal and the papyrus being Dr. Stillwell's property, I suspect you might have a different point of view."

Hala didn't respond.

"Nothing to say? Where are all your high-and-mighty principles now? You realize you are the cause of Helena's death. If you had approved our application to search for Nefertiti, as your superior promised to do, none of this would have happened. Helena insisted she needed more money to buy you off, but I knew it wasn't about money for you. It was about power and control. I refused, and she was furious. She threatened to disclose certain indiscretions to my wife. Surely you must see I could not allow that to happen. My wife is not well."

Dysart was practically raving. He waved the gun all over the place. Disgusting flecks of spittle caught in the corners of his mouth. He took out a linen handkerchief and wiped his face. The act appeared to calm him down a little. The boat bounced over a whitecap, and he almost lost his footing.

"I'm willing to put all that behind us. Helena promised finding Nefertiti would make us more famous than Howard Carter. Tutankhamen was merely an obscure boy-king. Nefertiti was one of the most beautiful and famous women in antiquity. Then Dr. Stillwell came along with her clues to finding Hatshepsut. Imagine the impact on the world of archaeology of discovering both Nefertiti and Hatshepsut."

He took the crystal out of his pocket again. "With this, and Dr. Stillwell's precious papyrus…" The wind shifted abruptly from the east to the west, sending the heavy sail boom sweeping across the deck. Dysart, not too steady in the first place, struggled to keep his balance. The boom hit him in the side. He juggled the gun and the crystal, and they both clattered to the deck. Hala dived for the crystal and clutched it to her chest. Cass and I scrambled for the gun, and she came up with it and pointed it at Dysart.

"Put your hands behind your head." Keeping her eyes on Dysart, Cass reached out to Hala. "I'll take that."

Hala turned the crystal over in her hands. She held it over the side of the boat and dropped it in the water!

I didn't think. I acted and dove over the side after it, in my clothes and heavy boots. The murky water closed in, and the first thing I noticed was an eerie silence. I was able to catch just a glimpse of sunlight reflecting off the dense glass as it sank in a straight line and landed on the river bottom in a puff of silt. I stroked as hard as I could with my shirt billowing around me and my boots dragging against the water. My hands found the bottom where I thought it had landed, and thank goodness I touched a hard, smooth surface. I grabbed it and headed up, praying my lungs could hold out. I broke the surface, pulled in a welcome gulp of air, and swam after the felucca.

Cass still had the gun aimed at Dysart, and Hala was sitting with her head in her hands. Omar reached over the stern and pulled me by my shirt collar into the boat. His eyes were as big as saucers. He wasn't able to understand English, but it was clear to him something very bad was happening. Cass took the crystal and gave me a quick hug with her free arm. "Hala, tell him to turn the boat around and take us back to the marina."

Hala said a few words in Arabic, and Omar climbed onto the log/tiller and turned the felucca into the wind. I knew enough about sailing to duck as the boat came about, but Dysart wasn't quick enough. The boom caught him again, and this time carried him in slow motion right over the edge and into the river.

We all rushed to the side of the boat. By the time we got there, he had disappeared below the surface. Cass and Hala and I stood motionless, waiting for him to come up. Seconds went by without any sign. Omar yelled, "Sobek!" Then a huge bloom of crimson erupted on the surface.

"What is it?"

Hala screamed, "Crocodile!"

I looked around frantically for something to use as a weapon, grabbed an oar from under the seat, and jabbed the water over and over.

Cass held me around the waist. "Ari, Ari, Ari. Stop. He's gone."

All the strength went out of my legs, and I sank to the bottom of the boat.

Cass carefully put the crystal into her briefcase. "Tell him to take us back, Hala."

Chapter Seventeen

A LOT HAPPENED IN the two weeks after the crocodile ate Lord Dysart. Now there's a sentence I'll bet no one from Beaufort, North Carolina ever wrote before. Anyway, when the truth came out about Helena Bendix bribing the Minister of Antiquities for a dig permit in the Valley of the Queens, like Hala said, the Prime Minister gave Hala her job back, and she expedited approval of our permit for the Hatshepsut dig. I figured she was trying to make up for throwing the crystal in the river.

With Dysart's confession, the police dropped the murder charge against Arthur Timms. Hala withdrew her attempted murder complaint against him, and he scurried back to England.

It turned out Mr. Hassan was working undercover with the National Police the whole time. Before the murder, they were already onto Dr. Bendix and Mr. Timms's black-market trading in antiquities. His proposal to me was an attempt to lure me into something illegal. So Hassan was never a suspect in Helena's murder as far as the police were concerned. He was a good guy not a bad guy. You could have fooled me.

Detective Inspector Salem got credit for solving Bendix's murder, and Beret Guy marched back to wherever he came from.

With the present-day murder behind us, we could start working on our original goal, finding Hatshepsut and solving a 3500-year-old murder. The night before our first trip to the Valley of the Kings, after a quiet room service dinner in our suite, we sat propped up in bed. I was trying to concentrate on *Egyptian Grammar: Introduction to the Study of Hieroglyphics*, and Cass had the papyrus spread out on her lap with a magnifying glass and a fancy electronic calculator. Her reading glasses were perched on the end of her nose, her dark hair framing her face in soft waves.

I gave up on hieroglyphics and slammed the book shut. She didn't look up.

I nuzzled her neck. "Your nose is very sexy."

"What? You find big noses sexy?"

"Your nose isn't too big. It's just right. It makes a statement."

She still didn't look up from whatever she was calculating.

"Show me what you're working on."

That got her attention. She scooted over and smoothed out the papyrus so I could see. "Senenmut wasn't only an able administrator and an architect. He was also an astronomer. Maybe the first one in recorded history. He left us a celestial chart showing the timing for how to use the crystal to find Hatshepsut. This chart on the papyrus is a duplicate of the painting on the ceiling of his tomb, which we're going to see tomorrow."

"But how will that work? Didn't he draw that picture thirty-five hundred years ago?"

"My dear, to the stars, thirty-five hundred years is just the blink of an eye. By my calculations, this time of the year we can find Hatshepsut around five in the evening, but to be safe we should have everything in place by two o'clock."

I picked up her left hand and kissed the tender inside of her wrist, where the pulse beat.

The edges of her mouth turned up. "Are you trying to distract me from my very important work?"

"Yes."

She rolled the papyrus, took off her glasses, clicked out the light, and pulled me on top of her. "It worked."

***

The next morning, we went down to the dining room for coffee and a roll. Sam stood at his usual station behind the reception desk. I wondered if the man ever slept. He bowed when we got off the elevator and hustled to show us to a table.

I opened my journal. "I want to write down the details of events over the last few days and close the chapter on Helena's murder so we can start finding Hatshepsut with a clean slate."

"Good idea."

"Did you know all along that Dysart murdered Helena?"

"No. I would have wagered it was Timms. He had the motive. Helena was trying to get him fired. We knew the killer was left-handed because the fatal blow came from the left and behind. Timms is left-handed."

"How did you know that?"

"When he checked his watch in the lobby, I noticed he wore it on his right wrist. A common practice of left-handed people. Another clue pointing to him, the bush okra seed I found in our carpet after the first robbery, probably came from his shoe. Helena complained he spent too much time cruising the market, where he could have picked it up."

"But then you got another note from the killer, after Timms was in police custody."

"That's right. At that point, it could have been Hala or Dysart."

"Or maybe Hassan?"

"Yes, but he would have been a stretch. No apparent motive, and he's right-handed. Hala and Dysart both had motives. Hala wanted to prevent Bendix getting her hands on Nefertiti. Dysart was desperate to keep Helena from telling his wife about their affair. He was afraid of losing his meal ticket. Helena was not a very beloved person. It turns out both Hala and Dysart are left-handed too. In fact, four are, Helena, Timms, Hala, and Dysart."

"But you said only ten percent of people are."

"I know. A very unusual coincidence."

"Now I remember. Hala had ink stains on her writing hand that night we went to her room. Her left hand."

"Yes. I didn't know Dysart was left-handed until we were on the felucca and he reached into his inside coat pocket for the crystal. He wears bespoke suits, specially made with the inside pocket on the right, convenient for a left-handed man. Then, of course, he confessed."

I had a flashback of Dysart going over the side of the boat and the big bloom of blood on the surface of the water.

Cass read my mind again. "You were very brave, diving in after the crystal." She shivered and rubbed her arms. "The crocodile might have eaten you instead of him."

"When Dysart fell over the side, Omar yelled, 'Sobek.' That's the crocodile god who punishes evil and protects the innocent, right? I think it was Senenmut's curse, and I don't have evil in my heart."

Cass touched my cheek. "No, you most certainly don't."

Chapter Eighteen

CASS HAD ARRANGED FOR Alfi to pick us up around noon. While we waited for him in the lobby, I power-wrote three letters to Mom and Gran. I felt guilty I hadn't kept up with my promise to write to them every day, but we had been pretty busy.

Cass sat staring into space and smoking.

I dropped the letters in the outgoing mail on Sam's registration desk and walked over and sat down next to her. "You must be beyond excited. If all goes well, you're about to become as famous as Howard Carter."

"Yes."

She didn't sound excited. She sounded like she was edging on one of her moods.

"What's the matter, Cass?"

"I keep thinking about what Hala said, about foreigners plundering the tombs, burning mummies for fuel in their campfires, satisfying our greed for fame and fortune, or even worse, just for the adrenaline rush of discovery. Senenmut risked his life, maybe even forfeited it, to hide Hatshepsut away for eternity. How do I have the right to disturb her?"

"Maybe you were meant to find her and tell her story."

"Maybe."

Alfi's van pulled up to the front door. I crawled in the back, picking my way over a ladder, shovels, a large portable spotlight, and a toolbox. We headed south on the boulevard skirting the Nile.

After two miles, we crossed the river. The landscape changed abruptly from a lush, green checkerboard of small farms to the yellow Sahara sands and craggy mountains of the Valley of the Kings.

We left the main road, and there it was against the cliff face–the Mortuary Temple of Hatshepsut. Cass touched Alfi's arm. "Stop for a minute. I never tire of this first glimpse."

I had studied photos, but mere pictures couldn't do it justice. The huge temple rose maybe a hundred feet from the valley floor. A ramp led up to the first and largest of three terraces. Across the front of each terrace were columns and giant statues of pharaohs, I guessed more examples of Hatshepsut advertising herself as the ruler of the two kingdoms. It looked totally different from the chunky Great Pyramid, more delicate, maybe because she was female? "It looks like a copy of temples in Greece."

"Except it was built a thousand years before the Parthenon. Picture the whole temple complex surrounded by gardens with exotic trees and reflecting pools." Cass checked her watch. "Drive on. We don't want to be late."

Alfi left the temple access road, turning right onto a one-lane, rutted dirt trail that dead-ended at the base of the mountain. We piled out, and Alfi unloaded the ladder and tools.

Cass pointed up the mountain. "That's Senenmut's tomb. That's where we're going." She shrugged on a vest and patted the pockets to make sure she had the crystal and papyrus. She added a flashlight and a small camera.

Alfi shouldered the ladder, and Cass and I gathered up the rest of the tools. Cass led the way, me in the middle, and Alfi came last. We struggled up the side of the mountain without any real pathway, snaking back and forth across the face. Loose gravel and sand made the going slippery as ice. I blessed my boots and concentrated on each step.

A barrier blocked the tomb's entrance. The sign, in Arabic and English, had a skull and crossbones. *Closed to the public. Danger. Trespassers will be prosecuted.*

Alfi took a crowbar from the toolbox and went to work prying nails from the barricade. He opened a gap wide enough for us to squeeze through with the tools. Beyond the entrance, the tomb was pitch-black. The mid-morning sun, rising from the east, didn't offer any light into the front entrance.

"Are we supposed to be here, Cass?" Me again, the rule follower.

Cass switched on her flashlight and stepped inside. "We have Dr. Tarek's approval. She's been very cooperative, trying to make up for impulsively tossing the crystal in the river. She regrets endangering your life. Stay close to me and watch your step."

Cass went first with the flashlight. I could touch both opposing walls of the narrow, sloping walkway that descended into the darkness ahead of Cass' light. Not a good time to feel claustrophobia. I focused on counting our steps. Thirty paces along, the walkway ended in a room ten feet square. Alfi switched on the spotlight.

Cass had told me the tomb was unfinished in antiquity. Senenmut was never buried there, but somehow, I anticipated we'd find something like the treasures Carter saw when he opened Tutankhamen's tomb. Instead, the room was completely barren. It seemed too modest a hiding place for history's greatest female pharaoh. Unfinished paintings filled the walls, depicting Senenmut leading processions honoring Hatshepsut and the gods. A picture of the night sky covered the ceiling with yellow five-pointed stars and astrological signs. This was why Cass said Senenmut was the first astronomer.

Cass turned in a circle, taking photos of the walls and ceiling. She unrolled the papyrus on the dirt floor, studied it for a moment, and trained her flashlight on a spot in the ceiling painting. "Right there, Alfi."

He dug a chisel and hammer from the toolbox and climbed the ladder. He found the seams around a stone the size of a small modern-day brick within the light from Cass' flashlight. He tapped lightly at first, then with more force. Each blow sent a shower of dust and sand settling onto Alfi's thick, dark hair. He paused often so Cass could climb a few steps up the ladder and inspect progress.

"I think we've got it, Dr. Stillwell." He put down the chisel and hammer and worked the stone loose with his hands. It fell to the ground with a thud and a column of five or six bucketloads of sand, rocks, and gravel emptied on Alfi's head and the ground around the ladder. He was lucky to hang on. Alfi sputtered, shook the dirt out of his hair, and climbed down the ladder. When the dust settled, a square shaft extended upward from the ceiling to the outside. Sunlight streamed from the hole in the ceiling onto the floor.

Cass took the crystal from a pocket in her vest.

Alfi climbed down and took Cass' hand to help her up the ladder. "You should place it, Dr. Stillwell."

Cass nodded. "Thank you, old friend." She climbed the ladder. Her hand shook as she fitted the crystal in the hole. A spangle of random points of sunlight, refracted through the facets of the crystal, filled the small room like an ancient disco ball.

"Now what?"

Cass checked her watch. "Now we wait as the sun moves across the sky. Let's study the ceiling and wall paintings while we wait."

I sketched in my journal while Cass taught a master class about the meaning of the celestial charts on the ceiling and the paintings and hieroglyphics on the walls. As the sun moved from east to west, the angle of outside light through the crystal changed. The spangles blended together to make bigger and fewer circles until there were only four left in a diamond pattern against the south wall.

Cass checked her watch. "Right on time." As she spoke, the four circles consolidated into one. "She's here." She pointed to a spot on the wall where digging would do the least damage to paintings. "Let's start small."

Cass and Alfi began chipping with hammers and chisels, careful to preserve as much of the plaster as possible. I collected debris. One of Alfi's blows broke through into some kind of cavity. There was a whoosh of hot air from the hole. They worked on the opening until it was about the size of an orange. Cass hesitated, took a deep breath, and went on all fours to train her flashlight inside.

"What is it? What do you see?"

Cass sat back on her heels and looked up at me with tears in her eyes. "I see a solid gold pharaoh's coffin." She handed me the flashlight and moved aside so I could look through the hole.

I felt a rush of adrenaline as the beam swept across the gleaming gold coffin. It was smaller than you would expect, only about six feet long, and it was sculpted in the image of a prone human figure. The light reflected off mosaics of colored glass and precious stones inlaid in the metal. The arms, folded across the chest, held the royal crook and flail. On the side of the coffin facing toward us, a giant incised wing wrapped the figure, embracing the body as if to protect it. "It looks small enough for a child."

"There would have been three coffins, one nested in the next. This was the innermost coffin. Pressed for time, Senenmut would have left the outer coffins in her tomb."

"Are you sure it's her?"

"We won't know with scientific certainty until we bring her out...but I feel it's her."

Alfi took the flashlight and looked inside the niche. "It's too heavy for the three of us. To be safe, we need ten strong men. You and Miss Morgan could go back into Luxor for the night and call my brother Ebo to recruit them. I'll stay on guard here."

Cass and I climbed down to the bottom of the mountain, careful to avoid starting a landslide in the loose rocks and dirt. We jumped in the van and headed back to Luxor. The late-afternoon sun reflected off the desert in shimmering waves. As we approached the river, the two-lane road skirted farms. We had the lane headed into the city to ourselves. All the donkey cart traffic was in the outbound lane, leaving the city empty of their loads of sugarcane. Cass hadn't spoken since we left the tomb, and I was reluctant to interrupt the silence, so I spent the time guessing what crops were growing alongside the road.

She rolled down the window and ran her fingers through her hair. "I'm thinking of leaving her hidden, of sealing the niche back up with the papyrus and crystal inside."

I jerked to attention. "But Hatshepsut told you in the Met that we have to find her to prove she was murdered for being a woman."

"What if that was my ego talking? Maybe Hala's right. If we remove her we're no better than any other tomb raiders."

"But what about Jessie Finn Markham and the 'unity of the past and present' and the value of studying how events in antiquity make us what we are today?"

Cass touched her necklace. "That's the conundrum. I wish Jessie were here now to tell me if Hala's right."

I pictured Hala during our first meeting in the lobby of the Winter Palace. She had said, "Hatshepsut belongs to the Egyptian people." What if it had been Egyptians who found her?

"Cass, what if you let Hala be the one who finds her?"

The van bumped onto the shoulder and skidded to a stop. Cass grabbed me and hugged me. "You are a genius! I'll call her in Cairo as soon as we get to the hotel."

She steered the van back on the pavement and got us to the Winter Palace in record time. We ran across the lobby, stopping only long enough to ask Sam to connect our phone in the suite with the Ministry of Antiquities.

I checked my watch. "It's late. Won't she have gone home already?"

"If I know Hala, no. She'll still be at her desk."

When we got to the suite, the phone was ringing, and Hala was already on the line. Cass motioned me over and held the receiver away from her ear so I could hear.

"You're working late."

"Yes, reviewing a backlog of expedition requests. How is your dig going?"

"Are you alone?"

"Just a minute." We heard the click of her office door closing. "I'm back."

"Hala, I think we've found something."

We heard a sharp intake of breath. "Have you found her?"

"I don't want to go into it on the phone. Can you come back to Luxor right away?"

"The next flight is tomorrow morning. It lands at seven thirty."

"We'll pick you up at the airport. Wear your field gear."

Chapter Nineteen

HALA, CASS, AND I stood in a semi-circle around the small hole in the wall of Senenmut's tomb. We could hear Alfi and Ebo shouting instructions in Arabic to the crew setting up tents at the base of the mountain.

Cass gestured toward the wall. "Well, go ahead and look."

Hala squatted in front of the hole, flicked on her flashlight, and peered inside. She gasped and fell backward on her butt. "It's her. It's the gold innermost coffin." She scrambled to her feet and grabbed Cass in a tight hug. I could understand her emotion, but that didn't stop the green-eyed monster of jealousy rearing his head.

For a long minute, the two of them just stood with their arms intertwined and stared at each other, two colleagues taking in the enormity of the discovery they had made. Cass broke the spell. "We won't know for sure until we bring her out. And even then, until we open the coffin. It may be someone else. It may even be empty." She picked up a hammer and chisel. "Let's make the hole a little bigger so we can both take a closer look. Ari, ask Alfi to bring the men up as soon as possible to get started taking down this wall."

***

The crew worked five days carefully removing the wall brick by brick. Ebo had chosen the men well. They moved steadily in harmony with each other with no wasted motion. They sang some kind of chant in Arabic the whole time. Hala said it was about encouraging each other to work hard and praising their bosses, Ebo and Alfi. Their ancestors might have sung a similar song building this tomb 3500 years ago.

I numbered and catalogued every stone so that Cass and Hala could restore the wall with the paintings intact once they had removed the coffin. Hala photographed the figures painted on the face of each brick, and Cass translated the hieroglyphics. The paintings were all about Senenmut's accomplishments in service to his beloved Hatshepsut. This guy was crazy about her. I began to wonder if the Japanese tour guide in the Met had been right after all about a love affair between the two of them.

At dusk on the fifth day, the coffin lay fully revealed in the niche. Alfi estimated it weighed about 250 pounds. He chose eight of the strongest and most careful workers to lift it and set it in a pine crate, specially built to protect Hatshepsut on her train trip to the Egyptian Museum in Cairo. They mounted the crate on a sled and hooked it up to an elaborate block-and-tackle pulley system. There was a tense moment when loose rocks, dirt, and gravel gave way under the weight of the crate, and Hatshepsut began to slide down the mountain before Alfi and the crew got it back under control.

Our last night in camp, Cass zipped the flap of our tent and crawled into her cot. "Is it possible to be too exhausted to sleep? I think I'll read awhile. Will the lantern keep you awake?"

"Not the light, but probably this pain under my shoulder blade."

She patted the side of her cot. "Come over here and let me rub it."

I crawled in and snuggled against her. She stuck her thumb in my back in exactly the right spot, and I jumped. "Too much?"

"No, good."

She massaged my back and kissed my neck, giving me goosebumps. "You go back to the US soon."

"Yes, I'll spend some time in North Carolina with Mom and Gran before I start classes at Columbia. I still have to find an apartment in New York and a job, and I'll probably need a roommate."

Her fingertip circled my nipple. "Will you miss me?"

I turned to face her. "Of course. What a question. I've wanted to ask what happens next between the two of us, but you've been so busy with Hatshepsut."

"I know, and the next few weeks are going to be even more hectic. We have to set up the lab in the basement of the museum, then clean and photograph every inch of the outside of the coffin and translate the hieroglyphics that cover the surface."

"You'll make a public announcement of the discovery."

"Yes. Imagine what that will be like. We'll be overrun by scientists, government bigwigs, and the public. Thank goodness that is Hala's department. We've agreed she'll be the public face, and I'll direct the science behind the scenes."

"When will you open the coffin?"

"Probably in two or three weeks."

"How can you wait? Aren't you anxious to see her?"

"Yes I am. I've imagined that day for a long time. Now it's soon to be here, but who knows what we'll find. It may be empty, or it may not be Hatshepsut."

"You'll find proof for the world that she was a pharaoh and evidence of how she died."

Cass yawned. Her eyelids drooped and then closed. "I hope you're right."

She was either too tired to talk about our future, or she was avoiding it. I tried to stay positive. I turned off the lantern and crawled into my cot.

Chapter Twenty

CASS AND I WALKED across the square from the Cairo Ritz-Carlton toward the wrought iron front gate of the Egyptian Museum. A Frenchman designed the Egyptian Museum in 1902, and Italians built it. No surprise the building didn't appear to have anything to do with ancient Egypt. Its color, an odd shade of terra cotta, reminded me of a flowerpot.

Hatshepsut was resting in a basement lab in the old building.

Cass put her hand on the small of my back. I couldn't tell whether it was for support or just connection. If it was for support, was it for me or for herself? As usual, even the most casual touch from her sent a tingle through my body.

I pointed to the line of visitors stretched around the corner waiting for the museum opening. "A crowd lining up already."

"Wait till the public finds out about Hatshepsut. Hala is doing a good job of planning for that. Thank goodness."

"Are you still okay taking a back seat to her that way? After all, you found Hatshepsut, practically in spite of Hala."

Cass touched the gold charm on her necklace. "That kind of recognition isn't as important to me as it used to be."

We showed our passes to an officer at the gate.

Inside the museum, to the left of the heavy double front doors, stairs descended to a dank basement that housed museum offices and restoration and research laboratories. A uniformed guard stationed outside the laboratory opened the door for us. The square space was as chilly as the inside of an icebox, with bare cement floors and walls. It smelled of freshly brewed coffee. In the middle of the room, surrounded by spotlights, the pine crate rested on two sawhorses.

Dr. Tarek and three assistants, wearing blue paper gowns, booties, rubber gloves, and masks, moved around the crate, adjusting the placement of the lights.

"Are we late?"

"I couldn't sleep, so I decided to get an early start." Hala's voice was muffled by the paper mask. "There's coffee in the corner and protective gear in that metal cupboard."

"I smell the coffee. Smells good."

"Yes, it covers up the musty odor." She turned in a circle. "Isn't this place dreadful?"

Cass nodded. "It is. Hardly fitting for a king. Here's some good news. I've had a wire from Dr. Zamboni. He's agreed to direct the forensic pathology. He's excited. He'll be here in ten days."

Hala pulled her mask down and grasped Cass by her shoulders and kissed her on both cheeks. "That's fantastic. He's eminently qualified to determine her cause of death. I know he's agreed to come because it's you who asked him." Hala beamed at Cass, her eyes filled with obvious hero worship.

Great. Now I had something else to obsess about—Cass and Hala becoming involved.

After a quick cup of coffee, Cass took a portable tape recorder and surgical magnifying glasses from her bag. It was the same brown leather case with a ruined lock that had held the clues to finding Hatshepsut. Cass simply hadn't taken the time to replace it. "Shall we get started?"

Hala held up a crowbar. "Lead on."

Removing the crate took all day until ten o'clock at night. Cass and Hala worked deliberately and slowly, careful not to damage anything. They photographed the coffin as each board was removed and recorded their discussion of the revealed carvings. The texts were spells from Hatshepsut's *Book of the Dead*, a roadmap for her journey through the afterlife.

I noted each step in my journal and drew the hieroglyphics. I remembered what Cass said that first day in the Met Museum. "When time comes to prove our case about Hatshepsut's murder, there must be no room for questioning the methods and results."

Finally, the solid gold coffin in the shape of the reclining pharaoh lay completely revealed. Cass motioned me forward for a closer look. She pointed out that the beard, a symbol of the divinity of the pharaoh, had been sculpted separately and attached to the chin. Curving lines of blue stone gave the illusion the beard was braided. The headdress was the one that you expect a pharaoh to wear, called a nemes. In ancient Egypt, only pharaohs were allowed to wear them.

The pierced ears, attached separately like the beard, further identified the image as female. Adult males didn't wear earrings. Her arms were crossed over her flat chest, No womanly curves. She held the royal crook and flail, inlaid with dark blue, turquoise, and yellow stones.

The image of Hatshepsut's face gave me the chills. It was otherworldly. The whites of her eyes, the dark pupils, and the heavy lines around the eyes were some kind of precious stones. Her full lips turned up slightly at the edges, giving the impression she was about to share an amusing secret.

"It's carved in her image, isn't it, Cass? She looks like she's about to—"

Cass interrupted me. "I know."

Hala took off her mask and gloves. "Let's call it a night." She let the assistants go and began switching off the spotlights. We tidied up the lab, turned off the overhead fluorescent light, and went out the door. I glanced over my shoulder. The coffin gave off a soft glow, somehow retaining the light. Creepy.

***

Every day and night for the next week, Hala and the assistants cleaned the surfaces with tiny, soft-bristled brushes, and Cass circled the coffin murmuring into her tape recorder. Finally, they were ready for a public announcement. The scientific community grapevine had already been working overtime. Egyptologists from all over the world called and sent telegrams of congratulations, asking for an invitation to be present at the announcement. Quite a change from the cynical denials when Cass' article put forth her theories about Hatshepsut.

On the weekend, television crews began hauling their equipment down the stairs and into the lab. The logos stenciled on their packing cases were from Egyptian national television and networks of other Middle Eastern countries, Europe, and America. By three on Saturday afternoon, the lab was transformed into a makeshift television studio, with spider webs of electric cords strung out across the floor to power video and audio equipment.

Hala stationed half a dozen assistants in white lab coats around Hatshepsut with orders to stand guard and protect her against accidental bumps or curious touches. TV technicians swarmed around the room, ignoring the coffin.

Museum staff set up rows of folding chairs for an audience of reporters, bureaucrats, politicians, academicians, and wealthy museum patrons. A podium with the national seal of Egypt sat to the right of the coffin. After a cocktail reception to encourage fundraising for the museum, Cass and Hala would answer questions from the guests and the press about the discovery and further research they planned.

At about four o'clock, guests started arriving. Waiters in short white jackets and black bow ties circulated with canapes and champagne.

Cass and I stood out of the way in a corner of the room and watched Hala, looking official in her lab coat, circulate through the growing crowd, shaking hands and making introductions. "As you said, Hala has taken to the job of being the public face of finding Hatshepsut."

"Yes, she has the temperament for it. Far better her than me. In a few days, Dr. Zamboni arrives and we open the coffin. That's what I'm looking forward to."

"You'll see her for the first time."

Cass gazed across the room to the gold coffin. "Yes, and I'm anxious to get started with the science."

"I'll just be in the way then. It's time I went back to Beaufort."

Cass crossed her arms and moved close to me so she could caress my waist in secret with her underneath hand. Very sexy. "You realize how important you've been to getting us here."

"You've told me that, and I love hearing it. But when you and Dr. Zamboni start your work, I'll be about as useful as a screen door on a submarine."

Cass laughed. "Another saying from your gran, no doubt. I'm looking forward to meeting her."

I crossed my fingers that meant Cass might soon be ready to think about the future of our relationship.

Chapter Twenty-One

TRAVELING FROM CAIRO, EGYPT to Wilmington, North Carolina, by way of Vienna, Austria and Washington, DC, took twenty-six hours. I could truthfully propose that, from the tarmac, every airport in the world looks about like every other one. After my landing in Wilmington, it was a four-hour Greyhound bus ride to Beaufort because we stopped at every Podunk junction along the way. Just before dawn, the bus pulled in at the Beaufort station, across from the Visitors' Bureau where we used to start the Pirates and Ghosts tours. "Aarg! Some rest peacefully, but some have unfinished business." That was my opening line when I conducted the tours back in high school.

The streetlights lining Ann Street flickered out as I walked past the United Methodist Church and the Old Burying Ground, crossed the street, and climbed the familiar steps of our front porch. There was a light on in the kitchen at the back of the house. I opened the front door, knowing they never locked it, and stepped into the smell of home. Funny, I was never aware of our house having a particular smell when I lived there, but after being away, it was unmistakable. Too bad you can't bottle that smell for times you need to feel safe and loved.

"Mom."

She came running from the kitchen with a dish towel in her hand. "Ariadne." She hugged me tight and turned us around in circles saying my name the entire time. "Let me see you." She held me at arm's length. "You're so thin, and your hair's lighter. You're putting something on it, aren't you?"

"No, Mom. Just lots of sun."

Gran came running out of her bedroom in her gown, robe, and slippers. "Ari." More hugs and more circles.

"Let her come into the kitchen, Mama." She herded me toward the kitchen table. "I'm making biscuits. I wasn't sure when you'd be here, but I thought I could always make another batch so they'd be hot if you came later. Sit down here, honey. You must be worn to a frazzle, traveling all that way." She pulled out a chair at the Formica-topped table.

Gran sat down across from me. "We saw your Dr. Stillwell on the television. It came on the six o'clock news. She's a smart one, that one, and a real looker, too. We watched for you, but you weren't on, were you?"

I glanced at the phone on the wall beside the back door. Cass made me promise to call her collect at the lab when I made it to Beaufort. She'd be watching the clock and checking my travel schedule. "No, I wasn't on TV. I was watching from behind the camera." I went to the phone. "I'm just going to make a quick collect call to let them know I've arrived safely."

Cass answered right away and accepted the charges. "I'm glad you called. Are you with your mother and gran?"

"Yes, they're right here. They saw you on TV."

"Tell them hello. Hala and the assistants are right here, too. Dr. Zamboni arrived this morning. We'll be opening the coffin tomorrow or the next day. Write to me at the Ritz." I could hear muffled movement as she put her hand over the receiver. "I miss you already."

"Me too. Goodbye." I hung up and took my seat again. Gran poured two cups of coffee for us.

Mom floured a rolling pin and attacked the biscuit dough. "How long can you stay, honey?"

That made me smile. It was always one of her first questions. "Only a week, Mom."

She shook her head. "Not very long then." She turned away and dabbed at her eyes with her apron. She stirred something in the ancient black cast-iron skillet on the front burner of the stove. "I'm making your favorite, sausage gravy for the biscuits."

I opened my mouth to recite my checklist of all the things I needed to take care of in New York before classes started at Columbia, but I stopped. How would that make Mom feel any better? Cooking sausage gravy for me was more likely to help.

Gran reached across the table and patted my hand. "Tell us all about your adventure. Start at the beginning and don't leave anything out. I could tell in your letters you were avoiding the juiciest parts."

Now that I was safely at home in the kitchen in Beaufort, there wasn't a reason to soft-pedal things. Mom set the plate of biscuits and gravy in front of me and joined us at the table. Between bites, I told Mom and Gran the whole saga, meeting Cass in the museum and watching her communicate with Hatshepsut, Helena's murder, Arthur Timms shooting at us, the crocodile eating Lord Dysart, and finding the gold coffin.

Gran poured us more coffee. "You little dickens. You solved a murder!"

"You surely did, but I'm glad we didn't know about it at the time. We'd have been worried sick."

"You could say I helped solve the murder. We were careful to keep ourselves safe." I had left out the part about me impulsively diving into the Nile to retrieve the crystal.

"What about the three-thousand-year-old murder? Is it Hatshepsut in the gold coffin? Did Dr. Stillwell prove she was murdered?"

"She's working on that now."

Mom went to get me another biscuit. "Honey, you should write about this in a story. This is better than Sherlock Holmes or Agatha Christie."

"Or *Columbo*," Gran said, ever the TV addict.

I scooted my chair back and patted my stomach. "That was great." The thirty hours of travel with very little sleep were catching up with me. "Is it okay if I take a short nap? Then maybe the three of us can talk some more or take a walk."

I took a shower with water as hot as I could stand it, then crawled between the cool sheets of my single bed.

My next thought was, *That can't be Jeopardy. Jeopardy doesn't come on till seven p.m. Surely, I can't have slept twelve hours.*

Then I heard Gran yell, "What is rhubarb?"

Turns out biscuits and sausage gravy can be a sleeping draught if you're worn out enough.

Chapter Twenty-Two

DOWNSTAIRS ON WEST 145ᵗᴴ Street, New York City trash collectors performed a concert, playing a garbage can percussion ensemble piece in front of our apartment building. I checked the dial of my glow-in-the-dark travel clock. 5:30. If I had been asleep, which I wasn't, the noise from the street would have sat me straight up in bed. I say bed. It was a convertible sofa in the living room of my old college roommate, Alison. Whoever designed this particular piece of furniture managed to build in a steel rod exactly where an average person's lower back would be. I wasn't getting a lot of sleep.

Alison agreed to temporarily let me stay with her, but the arrangement had some downsides in addition to the convertible sofa. She had three roommates in the four-bedroom apartment with only one bathroom. They weren't excited about another body in line for the facilities every morning. Also, Alison felt entitled to quiz me on the details of my affair with Eleanor. Her questions had an unwholesome quality. I guess Eleanor had been right about Alison's curiosity.

I was registered for two creative writing classes at Columbia, the fewest I could take and still be considered a full-time graduate student. After registration, I had two equal priorities: finding an apartment and getting a job. Cass had paid me generously for the summer, but the money wouldn't last long in New York City.

On the job front, I hoped to find something with a publishing house. Butler Library had a listing of all the publishers headquartered in New York City. I got a pocketful of change and started calling. Responses went from "I'm too busy to talk right now" to "Send us your resume." None of it encouraging.

For the apartment, I haunted the Columbia housing office. Everything was either too expensive or geographically undesirable. The office ladies got so used to seeing me, they just looked up and shook their heads when I walked in the door, indicating nothing new that fit.

The garbage truck gunned the engine and pulled down the street for the next movement of the concerto in front of the neighboring apartment building.

I turned on the lamp and picked up Cass' letter from the end table. It arrived my last day in Beaufort before I came back to New York, and I'd read it about a hundred times in the three weeks since.

It was on Ritz-Carlton Cairo stationery.

Dear Ari,

    We opened the coffin today. I imagined you here and holding your breath with me as we lifted off the lid. I won't keep you in suspense. It's Hatshepsut. Her head and shoulders are covered by a magnificent gold death mask, set with precious stones. The face on the mask is no doubt an idealized image of her at age twenty or so. Her wrappings are marvelously well preserved and are covered with tales of her triumphs as Pharaoh and spells to protect her soul through the afterlife. Even the most agnostic Egyptologist will acknowledge it is her.

    Our forensic pathologist, Dr. Luciano Zamboni, is set to examine her for clues to her life and cause of death. I've always had a preconception about the personalities of forensic pathologists, assuming they choose that medical specialty because they're more comfortable with dead tissue than living people. I suppose some would think that about archaeologists, too. Anyway, Luciano breaks the mold. He's a delightful, charming Italian from Naples. He's renowned for his studies of human remains from Pompeii and Herculaneum. He enlivens the atmosphere around the lab. He's a bit concerned about the outdated equipment we're working with—the x-ray machine is eight or nine generations out of date, but he assures us that he can make it work.

    The American Journal of Archaeology *saw our press conference, and the publisher contacted Hala last week to solicit an article. That hardly ever happens. Sweet vindication after the violent reaction to my "pulp fiction novel" two years ago. Your journal will be invaluable for helping me keep all the details straight once we start writing the article. Hala and I both expect you'll work with us and be listed as an author. That is, if you have time, of course.*

    I couldn't ask for a better partner than Hala. She works harder than anyone I've ever seen, and she's absolutely honest, sometimes to her own detriment. She treats me like a guru. It's quite a responsibility. She challenges me to be my best, too. Egyptology is very lucky to have a young person like her. She continues to manage the public relations part of our project, which is a relief for me.

    I miss you. I wish you had been here to share my first meeting with Hatshepsut. Please write to me as often as possible, and forgive me if I don't keep up my end during these next few weeks. I suspect things are about to get crazy. Whatever truths Zamboni finds will make big news in our community.

Take care of yourself,
Cass

I folded the letter and put it back in the envelope. I was glad to hear from Cass, but the talk of the wonderful Hala stirred up the old green-eyed monster in me again. Of course they were developing a special relationship, bonding over this momentous discovery. What could I expect, while I was halfway around the world? Would their relationship go beyond a professional one?

I tried to put it out of my mind. I took a shower as quietly as possible and decided to avoid making coffee, walk the mile and a half to Columbia for my seven o'clock class, and find a coffee shop on the way.

***

Approaches to Plot and Structure sounded dry, especially as a seven o'clock class, but the instructor was a moderately successful author who knew what he was talking about, and he actually seemed to enjoy teaching. Unexpected. That morning, we read aloud from our chosen works-in-progress. Mine was a murder mystery set in Egypt. I figured it could always be adapted as a *Columbo* script.

The bell sounded and I gathered my stuff and walked out of the classroom. Leaning against the wall across from the door was Cass.

I rubbed my eyes like they do in cartoons when they can't believe what's in front of them.

She smiled. "I should have told you I was coming."

"Don't speak." I grabbed her and pulled her outside to a bench under a tree. "How did you find me?"

"I'm still on the faculty. I got your schedule from the registrar's office."

"What are you doing here?"

"I'll tell you, but can I first just hold you a minute?" There was another of those long hugs that felt so perfect. We were both crying a little.

"Tell me what you're doing here."

"I have to bring you up to date. Zamboni found the proof that Hatshepsut was murdered. Choked to death."

"How?"

"There's a fragile bone under your chin right here." She caressed my neck and I got that feeling again you-know-where. "It's called the hyoid bone. It holds your tongue in place, and it's one of the reasons humans can speak. It hardly ever breaks because it's protected by the tough jawbone, but it almost always fractures when someone is murdered by strangulation. Hatshepsut's was broken in two places where her murderer's hands choked the life out of her."

"Her stepson?"

"That we may never know for sure. All this is secret until our article comes out in the *American Journal*. That's one reason I came back, to meet with my editor in Boston. But there's more. You know how outdated and sad conditions are at the Egyptian Museum in Cairo. In a delicious bit of irony, Lady Dysart sold her husband's New Kingdom artifacts and donated the proceeds, five million dollars, to the museum. The money will fund an institute for the discovery and preservation of Egyptian antiquity. Hala will be the director. That's the second reason I'm here. I'm meeting on Monday with the president of Columbia to propose a joint venture for the institute with a matching donation from the University."

"Will they do that?"

"Once I tell him about Hatshepsut, he will."

She took my hands. "But I haven't told you the most important reason I'm here."

I braced myself. This was where she was going to tell me that she and Hala had become involved.

"You remember when we captured Arthur Timms after he shot at Hala? He told us about a map he found to Nefertiti's tomb."

"Yes."

"And when Dysart confessed, the police released Timms to go back to England after Hala dropped her complaint against him."

"Yes."

"She put a condition on dropping the complaint. Timms gave her the map."

"Wow! You and Hala will search for her together."

"Hala will be busy setting up and running the institute. One thing I've learned in the last few months, I don't belong at fundraising cocktail parties or in a classroom or in an office. I'm meant to be in the field. What I want to ask is, will you come back to Luxor and search for Nefertiti with me?" She rushed on before I could react. "I know you might be reluctant to interrupt your graduate program, but wouldn't they give you a leave of absence or something, upon my recommendation?"

The clock tower began to chime nine, reminding me of the morning only a few weeks ago when I returned Eleanor's apartment key.

Cass took a big breath. "I know what you're thinking. I've been too busy...and maybe reluctant...to directly talk about our future together. Losing Jessie left such a big hole in my heart. I haven't been sure how much I have left." She took my face in her hands. "But I want to try with you."

She pulled a small black velvet bag from her pocket. "I brought you this. A bribe."

I turned the bag upside down and shook it. A gold charm in the shape of a cartouche on an impossibly thin gold chain fell into my palm.

"It's beautiful." I held the charm on the tip of my finger. "It's Nefertiti."

She nodded. "Will you come back to Luxor with me?"

I had no time for a pros and cons list. I belonged in the field with Cass. "Yes."

"Yes? You'll go?"

"Yes."

THE END

About Jane Alden

Jane Alden was born and raised in a small Mississippi River Delta community in Arkansas. Everyone in town knew everyone else—their parents, and their grandparents before them. Though her father was a life-long cotton farmer, the family lived in town rather than on the farm, the only class difference in the all-white, all-protestant hamlet.

After graduating from the University of Arkansas, she moved to California and taught seventh grade English in a small central valley citrus-farming community. When she was recruited on the phone at U of A, she looked up Porterville, California, on the map, and it was only about an inch and a half north of Los Angeles, but it turned out the culture was closer to Arkansas or Oklahoma than to the bright lights and big city she craved. After two years teaching, she moved to Los Angeles and began a career in health care management. After many lucky circumstances and thanks to wonderful mentors, she ultimately became Chief Executive Officer at Los Angeles Children's Hospital, a mountain-top experience. After running a big organization for eight years, she became an executive coach, working with successful executives who want to be better leaders.

Jane and her partner of thirty years live in a small town thirty miles east of metropolitan Los Angeles. Claremont is rare for a Southern California town, having a distinct downtown village area and discernable city limits. Their chocolate lab, Delilah, is the captain of the domestic ship.

Visit Jane's website at janealden.com to chat about lesbian stories, our experiences, and other interesting things. 'Like" her on Facebook at Jane Alden, email Janealdenauthor@gmail.com.

Connect with Jane:
Email: janealdenauthor@gmail.com
Twitter: @janealden5
Facebook: JaneAldenBooks

Cover Design By : Rachel George
www.rachelgeorgeillustration.com

Note to Readers:

www.ingramcontent.com/pod-product-compliance
Lightning Source LLC
Chambersburg PA
CBHW051145020726
47501CB00005B/1682